GLOWING PRAISE FOR B

Psychos

"Her laugh-out-loud antics will leave you wanting even more."

—*People*

"Babe Walker just gets me, which is really embarrassing. For me."

—Ashley Benson

"Babe Walker makes me want to be a better person."

—Elizabeth Banks

"A book so full of toxicity that I needed to see a healer when I was finished."

—Jake Shears

"Refreshingly egotistical . . . pithy, entertaining."

—*Kirkus Reviews*

"Babe's wildly popular Twitter persona, blog, and books are the creation of three actor-writer friends who use their creation's ludicrous observations and exploits to skewer the shallow ultrarich."

—*Booklist*

White Girl Problems

"Made me laugh a lot and cry a little. It's about time someone drew our attention to the devastating reality: white girl problems are all around us . . . absolutely hysterical."

—Susan Sarandon

"A snarky, satirical diary/memoir of how the poor-little-rich-girl goes from the lap of luxury to rehab after a $246,893.50 shopping spree meltdown at Barneys. . . . A confessed train wreck, [Babe] giddily invites you to stare. And just when you think you might finally need to look away, there's the impossibly startling—and hilarious—faux insight that keeps you hooked."

—*Publishers Weekly*

"A pop-culture send-up with a troubled material girl antiheroine . . . wickedly funny."

—*Kirkus Reviews*

"Amusing and laugh-out-loud funny."

—NewNowNext

"Do you ever go   and then realize you're $11 millio   nd love to laugh, *White Girl Proble*

—Examiner.com

ALSO BY BABE WALKER

Psychos: A White Girl Problems Book

White Girl Problems

AMERICAN BABE

A WHITE GIRL PROBLEMS BOOK

Babe Walker

(G)

Gallery Books

NEW YORK   LONDON   SYDNEY   TORONTO   NEW DELHI

G

Gallery Books
An Imprint of Simon & Schuster, Inc.
1230 Avenue of the Americas
New York, NY 10020

First Gallery Books trade paperback edition June 2016

GALLERY BOOKS and colophon are registered trademarks of Simon & Schuster, Inc.

For information about special discounts for bulk purchases, please contact Simon & Schuster Special Sales at 1-866-506-1949 or business@simonandschuster.com.

The Simon & Schuster Speakers Bureau can bring authors to your live event. For more information, or to book an event, contact the Simon & Schuster Speakers Bureau at 1-866-248-3049 or visit our website at www.simonspeakers.com.

Interior design by Jaime Putorti

Manufactured in the United States of America

10 9 8 7 6 5 4 3 2 1

Library of Congress Cataloging-in-Publication Data
Names: Walker, Babe, author.
Title: American babe : a White girl problems book / Babe Walker.
Description: First Gallery Books trade paperback edition. | New York : Gallery Books, 2016. | Series: White girl problems ; 3
Identifiers: LCCN 2016006073 | ISBN 9781501124846 (softcover : acid-free paper)
Subjects: LCSH: Socialites—Fiction. | Women, White—Fiction. | Self-realization in women—Fiction. | Self-actualization (Psychology) in women—Fiction. | BISAC: FICTION / Humorous. | FICTION / Biographical. | FICTION / Satire. | GSAFD: Humorous fiction. | Satire.
Classification: LCC PS3623.A3588 A84 2016 | DDC 813/.6—dc23 LC record available at http://lccn.loc.gov/2016006073

ISBN 978-1-5011-2484-6
ISBN 978-1-5011-2486-0 (ebook)

Dedicated to vaginas. Just, in general.

People are so codified—it's sad.

—JEAN PAUL GAULTIER

CONTENTS

AMERICAN BABE

ONE

Not Today.

"Are you okay?" A woman asked from roughly ten feet away, downhill from where I stood at the tip of the highest peak in Griffith Park. It completely took me away from my moment, which I resented. The sun had just begun to peer its glowing globe of majesty over LA's eastern skyline.

"Yes," I responded. "Nosy." I didn't look at her. I'd seen plenty already when I side-eyed her stomping up the hill toward me a few seconds earlier. She was hiking, she was blond, she was thin, she was worried that I might be getting ready to jump off the edge where I stood and end it all. I got it.

"Honey, can I ask, what are you doing?" she said with hesitation, putting a hand on my shoulder. She stood right behind me now. Awesome. Getting rid of her was not gonna be easy. I was dealing with an out-of-work, B-list fitness model who was for sure on her daily 5 a.m. hike and was probably super concerned about the beautiful, young girl she just found standing at the edge of a steep fucking cliff, about to jump.

"I'm fine. You can go about your hike. Really."

"Are you sure?"

"Yes, lady," I said.

"You don't need to do this."

"Okay, relax, you don't even know—"

"You're a beautiful girl."

"Thank you for seeing that beneath this neoprene face mask. You obviously have a great eye for eyes," I genuinely offered.

"I have a daughter and, you know, she's going through a rough patch right now, too. And I've been there before. Trust me. I used to live in Vegas."

"Whoa. Ew. Okay. Stop. I'll explain."

"Yes, talk to me, mama. Let's talk this out."

"Well, first off, don't call me or other people 'mama.' It's insulting."

"I just think it's a cute thing to call my girlfriends."

"Am I your girlfriend?" I said, trying to sound as nice as possible.

"I . . . guess . . . not."

She looked genuinely hurt. Not my problem. I mean, I was the one offering her helpful advice.

"So," I started, "this story begins on the day I auditioned to be Tom Cruise's new wife, which was weird as fuck, but it was also a major big-deal day that in a strange way affected the rest of my life. Tom does that to people, I guess. It was post all the Kidman divorce drama, and Tom and his team were screening several young actresses and non-actress-but-still-attractive people—like me—for the role of his 'wife.'

"I'd been a fan of his since the first time I saw *Rain Man* at age four, and I even thought he always seemed kind of cool and amazing and weird and rich, but I didn't exactly see it working between Tom and me. However, I wasn't about to pass up the opportunity to meet him for dinner at a castle in Portugal, where he was filming something or whatever. I'm not much of a European castle girl because normally the water in the showers is soft water, which is bad for my skin and hair, but this one was so breathtaking that I didn't even mind the water. It sat on the gorgeous Atlantic coast, and we ate in a room with window-lined walls looking out at the bluest, most endless ocean I'd seen maybe ever. I don't remember what we ate because I just don't, but it was delicious. Tom looked handsome in the face, wore a simple white tee and jeans, brown scuffed Prada boots, and smelled like heaven took a shit all over his body. I asked him what cologne he was wearing and he said he wasn't wearing any. So mysterious. So Tom."

"So Tom," said the ex–fitness model, whose name I decided was Mel.

"My lawyers have strongly advised me not to repeat exact content from the conversation Tom and I had that night. I can say, though, that it never went past just talking between us. But I think I can tell you about one of the things we talked about that night. I mean, I had to sign a nondisclosure agreement, but we all know those aren't real, don't we?

"On that blustery night, tucked away in a villa on the majestic Portuguese coast, Tom shared with me one of his 'passions in life': squirrel diving. Most people have never heard of it, let alone tried it because it's so dangerous and chic. Squirrel diving is an extreme sport that requires the diver to don a highly technical suit made of fiberglass, neoprene, and stingray skin. Built into the armpits is a sheet of webbing, like a flying squirrel, giving it its name. Duh. How *Mission: Impossible* is that? He said never to try it because I would 'probably die.' His concern was sweet but only made me want to do it immediately. If you don't want me to try something, especially a drug, don't entice me with the threat of death, Babe rule number one.

"Well, a few years passed by, Tom married Katie Holmes, Katie Holmes divorced Tom, I lived my life, shopped a lot, went to rehab, kept being a mess, traveled, wrote two books, fell in and out of love with my soul mate, Robert, and ended up back in LA."

The woman's expression hadn't changed since I started my story.

"So, so, so cool," she said.

I looked at her for a long time and thought about the daughter she probably has, sitting at home thumbing through Tinder, alone.

"So I'm gonna go now," I said, turning toward the vast view of Los Angeles, mentally preparing to jump. She still stood like a statue, lifeless, roots a mess.

"So why did meeting Tom change your life?" she asked.

"Oh, because now I'm conquering one of my fears slash completing a goal of mine that I've had for years. I've always wanted to jump off a cliff and now that I've spoken with Tom about it in Portugal and watched a few chic yet informative YouTube tutorials filmed in the Swiss Alps and bought the suit and shit, I'm ready. So I'm gonna need you to back away a little bit because I need some room for my running start."

I walked backward five or six steps until I had given myself enough runway before the edge of the canyon, pulled my goggles around my head tight with a snap against the back of my hair, and stretched my arms wide to check for tangles or folds in the underarm webbing of my suit. I was good. I was ready. I'd kind of done this before, I could do it again.

"You're fucking Babe Walker," I whispered to myself inside the tight and echo-y cavern of my fiberglass helmet. "You can fly."

I took a sprinter's position, felt the sand push against the pads of my fingers, looked out over the city one last time, and shot myself forward with every bit of strength I had in my well-toned core, butt, and thighs. After a few aggressive yet graceful steps, I was off the edge. Luckily, it was windy as fuck that morning, and I was immediately lifted skyward by a gust of generous breeze. God clearly wanted this to work for me, too. I could hear the hiker lady screaming behind me. She obviously couldn't understand what was happening. She didn't know that this was my thing. I had this.

The trick to squirreling is keeping your entire body stiff as a board and light as a feather, à la *The Craft*. With a slight bend at my elbow and a cupped swimmer's hand, the air supply was able to tuck itself right under my cute, almost weightless body. I'd call it an extreme sport, but I don't do "sport." I will say, however, it's extremely body-affirming. I mean, you literally have to be able to float. This is chic, no?

I may be under the assumption that most people's lives are more boring than not boring, but I doubt you've ever done anything as exhilarating as this, besides maybe cocaine. So I can't expect you to understand the mind-splitting thrill of literally soaring above Los Angeles. It's EVERYTHING. From about 1,100 feet above the ground I could see the In-N-Out Burger where I threw a Sprite in a blind date's face for ordering me a Sprite, and the movie theater on Hollywood Boulevard, where I gave the one with a ponytail from One Direction a hand job. The Scientology Centre was the size of a Fendi Baguette from up there, and I even saw the acting studio where I'd taken an improv class for fifteen minutes before getting frustrated, screaming "Clowns!" and walking out. A very *This Is Your Life* moment for me.

The birds flying past me were probably wondering, *What the fuck*, but I spiritually greeted them all with an open heart and thanked them for sharing the sky with me, just a girl with the simple dream of getting high on adrenaline and being more like my role model, Tom.

I leaned my right shoulder to the ground just the slightest bit to set my trajectory westward toward the direction of my house in Bel Air. Well, more specifically my backyard, which would also function as my landing strip. Side note: Do you have a landing strip of hair above your vagina? If so: Don't. I could begin to see the northeastern border of the neighborhood and followed the streets with my eyes until I saw my house and the yard, waiting for me.

I heard flapping sounds near my left-side ear but couldn't see anything. The sound was loud and scary and so not cute. And it was only getting louder by the second. I couldn't move away from it even though I wanted to because the thing about squirreling is you have to let the wind take you, more or less. A lot like life and anal sex. Then a hard whack slapped down across the top of my head. In a flurry of brown and white feathers and body and legs, I made out the form of a monster-sized turkey/eagle/hawk bird next to me, and it was trying to attach.

"Are you FUCKING JOKING?!" I screamed. My voice reverberated inside my helmet, which all of a sudden felt more like a cage.

Keep your form. Keep your form. KEEP YOUR FUCK-ING FORM. Tom says if you never lose form, you'll never lose control. What the fuck, though? This is insane. I hate everything about this.

The albatross, or whatever it was, was now fully attached to my neck and no matter the quaking and shimmying I did to get shake it off, this mad bird queen was going nowhere.

I was going down.

I'd lost control.

I'm sorry, Tom.

The city got closer and closer by the second. My vision blurred with the fact that I was already dead. This was it. I guess I've lived enough? I'd done everything I wanted to do in my short, blazing life span besides wear an armadillo McQueen hoof bootie to church in Rome and sleep with Leo DiCaprio. I'd have to come back and do those things in another life, I guess. I found peace in the moment. I had no choice. In my head I could hear Yo-Yo Ma playing Ennio Morricone's *The Mission*. I guess this was my death music.

The ground was like a wave swell, closing in on me. Almost as if it was about to break and crash, falling onto me, and not the other way around. Wait, that's a beautiful image. Then . . .

NO.

NOT TODAY.

NOT! TODAY!

I'M NOT DONE YET.

I'd come so close to dying sooooOOOO many times over the years (heat exhaustion, overshopping, overdieting, over-Pilatesing, stalkers, plane crashes, my failed and sloppy arson attempt), and there was no reason I couldn't pull myself out of this.

"You're fucking Babe Walker. You can fly!" I shouted, sharply twisting my shoulders.

With a deafening squawk, the bird let go!

But nope, that didn't exactly help the cause. The problem was, I was then upside down with my back to the surface of the earth, then belly-down again; I was literally torpedoing. With a quick glance I saw that I was headed toward a one-story building in Westwood that had lots of glass windows. *Oh God, please don't let me die in a donation-based yoga studio*, I thought. Just no.

I opened my mouth wide and from the literal seafloor of my soul released the loudest Mel Gibson as William Wallace battle cry. The next thing I remember is the sound of glass shattering, women screaming, a sea of aggressively bright yoga clothes, and the light aroma of eucalyptus. I figured this was hell.

TWO

Stop Being So Nice. It's Rude.

My gaze was stuck on one of those oddly shaped greige spots that form on gridded hospital/office building ceiling material. It looked like a sick pit stain, leaking its way from the corner of the foam ceiling section. I thought this was supposed to be a nice hospital? I barely remember getting here but I do recall the bedsheets being softer than I expected when I was lifted in by the two strong EMTs that brought me here. That yoga studio situation was a mess. I mean, I feel bad for fucking up their entire business probably for a long time—they'll need new windows and mirrors and the people in the class are most likely traumatized and will never return—but I also didn't feel bad. I was alive, and my face didn't need to be reconstructed, that's what mattered.

"NURSE!!!" I screamed.

Honestly, the service in this hospital . . . it's fucking deplorable. Hospitals should be more like hotels. Make us feel like it's a privilege to be injured or sick, not a punishment. Anyway, I could tell I'd been sleeping for at least fifteen hours because the morning sun was up, and I felt less dead and more Babe. When I'd arrived at the emergency room I'd been diagnosed with a broken rib, but I felt it best to supplement the doctor-prescribed Vicodin with some Babe-prescribed Xanax and Percocet from the emergency stash that I always keep with me. Comas are chic, and comas of the medically induced nature help the body heal.

"Oh, you're awake?" said the rabbit-faced nurse, who I kind of remembered from before I passed out. She had red hair and red scrubs and red Crocs. I could actually get behind her solid-color-blocked look—for her, not for me.

"I'm really, really, really, really, really, really, really, really, very thirsty. Can you grab me a San Pellegrino? Room temp, if poss, with one ice cube. Thanks so much. I'm going to give this experience a glowing review on Yelp. It's really been extraspecial. Do you guys do mani/pedis here?"

I started to realize as these words were coming out of my

mouth that I was still pretty high from the drugs. But I was too high to stop talking.

"Well, Barbara," she said, reading my name off of her clipboard. "We don't have Pellegrino here at the hospital."

"Please call me Babe. Barbara is a name that was given to me at birth as a sick joke. My dad is a monster for naming me Barbara. Perrier will be fine. And some down pillows if it's not too much to ask."

"This is a hospital, darling. Not the Ritz."

"Ew . . . Thank God it's not the Ritz. The Ritz is fucking sick."

"Well we don't have anything other than apple juice or fruit punch in a can, and the pillow you have under your head at the moment is the only kind of pillow we use."

I made a face that was 50 percent smiling and 50 percent sad face. Whatever. It made sense in my head at the time. I was high, get off me.

"Is my doctor available to chat?"

"Yes. Dr. Chen will be in with you in a moment."

"Dr. Chen sounds like he's hot."

"She is."

"Even better. Send her in."

When I sat up a bit and reached for my phone on the bedside table, I realized that my rib was incredibly sore. Side note: When I was younger I fantasized about having a couple of ribs removed to create a slimmer waist contour, but my dad wouldn't let me do it, and then a friend of mine's mom did it the next year and died, which obviously changed my view on the procedure. But it did occur to me in this moment that maybe my rib had been broken in such a way that it would achieve the aesthetic I'd always hoped for, even if it was just on one side.

So I just tried my best to get comfortable in a seated position. The room was nice, for a hospital, I guess. (It actually reminded me of a W Hotel room from 2005 that I once stayed in in Westwood when I was having my dad's house smudged of spirits and ghosts after a bad breakup with my high school boyfriend.) Someone had sent me a huge bouquet of flowers, but it was on the other side of the room so I couldn't tell who they were from. But they were hydrangeas, so it was probably from my dad and his fiancée, Lizbeth. She's obsessed with hydrangeas, and I told her that I loved them, too, a few years ago when I was buttering her up to convince my dad not buy this house in Cabo from George Clooney. It's just not that cute to buy a house from someone more famous than yourself.

I also noticed a huge box of chocolates on the bedside table and assumed they were from my best friend, Genevieve. If you've ever been to LA, you've seen her dancing or sleeping on a banquette at the Chateau. She's always been there for me, since I met her as a kid, but she'd also probably orchestrate my assassination if she was jealous enough about a new bag or a recent lay with a guy she liked. That slut thinks of everything.

"Miss Walker?"

I looked up to see a really hot doctor-man standing before me.

"Are you Dr. Chen?" I asked. These drugs were really doing a number on my vision.

"Nope. I'm Dr. James Hunt. I'm the attending on duty. How are you feeling today?"

His energy was exactly Robert's; it was bewildering.

"Do you know Robert?"

"Not sure I do. Who is that?"

"Robert. My ex. He's a doctor, for sports."

"Don't know him, unfortunately, but how are you feeling right now?"

"He's really a great guy. I think I miss him right now, which is weird because I was the one who ended things. It was just boring, you know?"

"Are you feeling woozy?"

"I'm feeling fine. Robert used to say 'woozy' all the time. So weird. Anyway, I wanted to get engaged and he wasn't asking and then finally he wanted to go pick out a ring with me, but he should just know what ring I want, so then I was just annoyed at that point so I was like completely over it and then I moved out."

"I think you should get some more rest, Barbara."

"Babe. I'm fine, though."

"Okay, good. How is your abdomen feeling? You had a pretty bad break on your twelfth rib. You really should not be using a squirrel suit within the Los Angeles city limits. It's very dangerous, and I'm pretty sure illegal."

"Oh, so you're a doctor and a lawyer?"

"I'll have Dr. Chen check back in on you in an hour or so. Good luck with your boyfriend."

As the doctor-man left, I saw an email from Donna pop up on my phone. Donna Valeo is my real mom, my bio-mom. She left me with my dad when I was born, only to run away and become a supermodel. Her identity was kept from me "in my best interests," but then in a weird twist of fate, I ended up rooming with her wife, Gina, at rehab a few years back—Donna came to visit Gina, everyone put the pieces together, and the truth was out.

From: DONNA (d.valeo7979@gmail.com)
To: Babe Walker (babe@babewalker.com)
Subject: Question

Babe,

Sorry this is so last minute but my father (who is your grandfather) is having his 80th bday in Maryland this Saturday. I'm gonna take the train down from NYC tomorrow. Can you meet me? Would be nice to introduce you to your family. You can stay with me at my sister Veronica's house with us and her kids Cara and Knox, or get a hotel if that's too much.

Anyway let me know if you can make it. Didn't decide I was going until 5 minutes ago.

Love,

Donna

I mean. I didn't even know who she was until I was twenty-five and since then we have literally hung out four times. So the chance of me going to fucking Maryland to be with her and her strange suburban family were negative-1,000 percent.

Maybe I did need more sleep because I was starting to feel extremely uncomfortable. My ribs were vvvv sore, but I was also wearing a hospital gown made of sandpaper and strings and I hadn't washed my hair in about forty-eight hours. SOOOOO, I had a choice: either get my fucking shit together, which would mean showering and having a vintage Lanvin nightgown messengered to the hospital so I could feel comfortable, or I could just take another five Vicodin and pass out for a second full day. Unfortunately, neither of those things was going to happen because, as I finished that thought, my dad and Lizbeth walked into my hospital room. They had thoughtfully grabbed my huge Goyard tote and filled it with my laptop, iPad, and all of the magazines that must have been sitting on the desk in my room.

A little info on my dad/Liz/me/us: When I decided that I was bored and annoyed in my relationship with Robert, I moved back into my dad's guesthouse. My father, who is an attorney to the A-list celebrities of the world, has always been a serious workaholic. But this past year, he has kind of scaled it back about 10 to 20 percent. He is spending more time and traveling a lot with Lizbeth, who is also a workaholic. She created this kind of chic yet kind of basic fitness-lifestyle brand and has been really successful, and as much as I don't love that she is only eleven years older than me, she is genuinely one of the nicest people in the world. She honestly does not need to be as nice as she is. It's almost rude of her. But alas, they really love each other and she makes my dad happy, and he's working less, and they don't seem to care that I'm twenty-seven and still living at the house, without a job. So it's whatever.

"There she is," my dad said in his version of a quiet voice, which is a normal-volume voice for everyone else. "How are you feeling, love?"

"Hi, Dad. I'm fine."

"So? Dear? What in the bloody fuck of all fucks were you thinking jumping off a mountain?"

"Dad, please don't ask me *why* this happened. This obviously happened because God hates me."

"Oh, stop that. Do you want me to see if there's a case against the flight suit manufacturers?"

"No, Dad. It's fine. I don't have the energy for a lawsuit right now, nor do I feel like investing the time it'll take to research and purchase an entire set of court looks. Just leave it alone."

"So happy to see you awake," Lizbeth chimed in. "We came to visit you when we first got the call, but you were asleep by the time we got to the hospital. I cut you those hydrangeas from the cutting garden."

"Thanks, guys. Really sweet of you, really. But I'm fine. You know me. I can get through anything. Luckily I don't have any work or personal obligations at this point in my life, so this injury won't really cause any problems for anyone but me."

My dad seemed satisfied with that answer but he may have been trying to move things along, because he gave a little smile and then pulled his vibrating phone out of his pocket.

"I've got to take this, ladies. Excuse me."

"He's in the middle of a big case?" I said.

"Yeah. Michael Jackson estate. Still."

"Cute."

"So . . ." Lizbeth looked nervous, which made me feel nervous because she is never nervous.

"So?"

"Are you okay, Babe?"

"What do you mean? I'm in the hospital. I'm as good as one can be considering I just sustained massive internal injuries due to a high-impact aerial accident while accomplishing a major life goal."

"I know, but are you okay?"

"I'm still not sure I understand the question."

But I totally understood the question. I was fully aware of what Lizbeth's vibe was in this moment. She wanted to get real with me. This is what she does for a living. She gets people to talk about themselves and improve upon who they are. But I was not about to have this conversation right now.

"Babe, you know, this is what I do for a living. I help people find their true path and help them realize their dreams. You have so much potential."

Here we fucking go. I'm just going to listen. I'm not going to say a goddamn word until she is completely done.

"We're not that different, you and me. I too was pretty lost when I was your age."

Of course you were lost. You lived in actual Wisconsin, Lizbeth. And we are not that alike because you are fucking my dad.

"I was jumping from job to job, relationship to relationship. I had no passions."

Okay, first of all, I couldn't be more passionate. I am passionate about last fall's collection from The Row, passionate about not having kids until I'm thirty-five, passionate about making the lives of my friends more fun and making the lives of my frenemies more uncomfortable.

"You tried to work at your dad's law firm, which lasted a week. You started a fashion line that folded. You worked at *Vogue* for a minute, you even wrote two books that were successful, but you never even seemed that passionate about being a writer."

This bitch.

"Like, Babe, what is your motivating force? What is your true passion? What makes you happy? You left Robert in the midst of what seemed like a very healthy relationship. Why? What is driving you to make those kind of choices?"

This person genuinely does not get who I am.

"I genuinely don't understand who you are. Like, you are one of the most confusing individuals. You're beautiful, extremely intelligent, driven when you want to be, effective in getting what you want."

Now you're starting to make some sense, Liz.

"But somehow the most misguided human being I've ever met. What is your mantra? What do you want out of life?"

OMG, ask me *one* more question that doesn't have a real answer, and I'll lose it.

"I just don't want you to avoid the question of how you got to this place, mentally. What do you need to feel secure in your life? What does Babe need to be truly happy?"

Never speak again.

"I know this may feel like a lot to deal with right now, with you being in a hospital, but sometimes these rock-bottom moments are the only way to shift your journey toward a healthier path. To find a new mantra. I believe in you."

I sat there in silence for a solid minute trying to craft a scathing response. This was a challenge because truthfully, it was impossible to miss the fact that she was speaking from the heart and actually trying to help.

"It's funny that you bring all this up now," I said. "I'm kind of like ten steps ahead of you on this one. I've been thinking the same exact thing for a while now and I really actually do know what the fuck I'm doing with my life, coincidentally. I've just accepted an invitation from my real mother to go visit our extended family in scenic Maryland, for my maternal grandfather's eightieth birthday celebration. Been feeling like I need to reconnect with my roots slash past in order to figure out where I'm going in the future. You know?"

"Yes. I do. That's amazing, Babe. Good for you."

Lizbeth seemed genuinely impressed with my answer.

"Yeah. It is really good for me. I'm truly looking forward to it. I've heard Maryland has really chic . . . um . . . crustaceans."

FUCK ME.

THREE

Why Would I Be Your Babysitter?

"I'm going to the airport. Terminal Seven. United," I said to the Uber driver as I hopped into her black SUV a couple days later.

"Sure," she said, smiling back at me.

I love a lady driver. I normally ask them about cabbies' rights and about women in that workplace, in the city, safety issues, etc. I'll really go in sometimes. But not today. Today I was in a somber mood.

"I'm gonna close my eyes now and meditate until we get there, so please don't ask me anything or make any loud noises with your mouth or turn the car sharply. I so appreciate it. Thank you so much, you're the best. Thank you."

"Sure," she said again, in the same tone but without the smile.

I was mad.

And sad.

And bad.

And glad.

Just kidding, I wasn't glad, or bad, really, I just got caught up with the rhyming.

But seriously, I refused to sit there anymore and handle the dramatics. My family was acting like a soap opera. Like, what is everyone's damage? Because I just don't get it. I feel like I'm so super chill and really, really try to inspire an atmosphere of chillness around me, yet my family is always on level ten when they don't even need to be. No one died, right? Right? Right, Lizbeth? I'm not some fucking murderer or degenerate running willy-nilly through Los Angeles. I'm not hopeless. I don't need direction, okay? I Googled "Maryland," and once I saw that it was definitely a continental United State, I booked a direct flight. I haven't flown internationally since the Malaysian flight disappeared—I refuse to go out like that.

I was going to be with my real family, a simple group of simple people who would probably be so confused by every thread my of being that they'd have no choice but to accept me for what I am: not simple. And I was genuinely excited to meet these normals, so I'm not using "simple" as an insult. There was no prejudging going on. I left LA with an open mind. In fact, a heavy pour of simplicity is what I needed in my life.

We got to the airport annoyingly quickly, which probably meant that I needed more meditation than I got. I hate when I can't get enough in. Meditation is actually horrible, don't do it, or do, I don't know, meditate on it and then decide. But I was there: LAX. I was on my cute way to cute Maryland, and this was happening. The flight was bumpy, but I will say the flight attendants in first on a United flight to Maryland are way more put together than you'd imagine. The tallest and modeliest of them was doing a brown YSL lip with her aubergine hair top-knotted to absolute death.

When I slurred (1.5 Xanax and a glass of gin), "You're too chic for this," she looked blankly at me, then smiled and exited the scene. Don't blame her for being caught off guard, it was challenging because it was true.

The airport smelled weird and dealing with the woman at the rental car place was tough. I'm sincerely sorry for anyone that's ever had to rent a car.

I made it to the address in Donna's email at around 7:30 p.m., and it was getting dark. I'd forgotten about the east coast being depressing with its short days. I slowly cracked the Chevrolet Malibu's window and peered out. The house was on a street with other houses that looked the same as each other, a variation on chimney placement or door color here or there. It felt simple. And . . . safe.

I grabbed my royal blue Anya Hindmarch maxi tote (chic, holds everything, AND features a large, perforated smiley face across one side: a symbol that I had arrived in peace) in one hand and my rolling Goyard carry-on in the other and clomped my way up the path toward the front door. DING DONG DING DONG rang the doorbell. "They need to change that sound," I whispered softly.

The door swung open, and I was greeted by a male child.

"Come on in!" he said as if I were the camera crew for his *Cribs* episode. I stepped back, trying to process the excessive and, mind you, blind hospitality, and noticed something . . .

"I'm sorry, male child, but are you wearing the Dior Fusion sneaker in navy with black sequin appliqués right now?"

"I'm not clear, is that a rhetorical question? You're looking at them," he stated, truly confused, as if to ask if I was partially blind and needed help identifying the shoe.

"Wait," I uttered.

"Wait what?"

"Wait, like, who are you?"

"What do you mean, who am I? I live here."

"Are you me?"

"No . . . " he said with a tilt of his head. He looked

concerned now. "Who are you?" he asked. "You're not the babysitter tonight? Danielle or whatever?"

"What? Does it look like that word could be my name? And why would I be your babysitter? That's a LOLZ."

We looked at each other.

"Are we fighting?" I asked His Highness.

"She's obviously not the babysitter. She has a suitcase," said a girl walking up behind him, wiping her hands with a dishrag. Oh, there's no help here. She was cute in the face for a teenage girl, but her entire outfit was a size small for her build, which was not bad, in a SoulCycle way. "How can we help you?"

"I'm Babe Walker."

The boy's eyes lit up. He knew that name.

"No fucking way," the girl said.

"Yes fucking way. Do you guys know who I am?"

"You're Donna's daughter," said the boy, whose freckly face was now wrapped in a huge smile. "Babe Walker."

"Right. That's my, um, name."

I felt a little weird because I didn't know if he was just cheesing to meet his first cousin for the first time and also realize that she's an image of freshness and glows with a bright aura of grue (green/blue), OR . . . was he a superfan of my books? That could be cute, I guess. I was shocked ten-year-olds could even read. My memory of that age is shot.

"You're Knox, right? So that must mean you're Cara," I said to them, proud of myself for remembering their names.

"Yep, exactly. And you're *the* Babe Walker. Wow," Knox said kind of loudly. "This is cool."

"He reads your books or whatever," Cara said, uninterested. She clearly did not read my books because if she had she'd know not to wear a teal spaghetti-strap tank top. Knox, on the other hand, was giving me a complete fashion look. An almost minimal/Japanese approach to a classic ten-year-old laissez-faire aesthetic. And the Dior sneaker just slayed me. There was an undeniable and immediate connection between the two of us. I guess we did have some of the same blood.

Cara finally asked me if I wanted to come in, and they showed me the house. It was basic, but I wasn't there to judge. I told them about Donna's email and how I need family in my life for it to be complete and they told me blah blah blah where they went to school and what their favorite colors were, and it was a perfectly cute getting-to-know-you sesh. Soon it became clear that their babysitter was not showing up. Who does that? The kids could've literally starved if I hadn't dropped from the sky. And their mom, my aunt Veronica, whom I'd still never met at this point, was on a night shift at a hotel nearby where she worked the front desk. The kids told me she had two jobs or something insane like that and their dad wasn't really in the picture.

"Do you know where he lives or if he's alive, et cetera?" I asked them, sitting at the kitchen island having a glass of water. I was parched and needed a liquid snack but the only other beverage options were Diet Coke, lemonade, milk (from a cow not an almond or a soy or a rice or even a hemp), and . . . hold on tight for this . . . Yoo-hoo.

"Yeah, Dad lives out in Virginia," Knox told me. "He calls a couple times a year. He's a salesman of some kind or a recruiter maybe? We don't really know. But he travels a lot. Not to Maryland, though."

"That's so douchey," I said.

"We think so, too," he said.

"Okay!" I blurted, trying to change the subject as quickly as possible. "So it looks like I'm the babysitter tonight because yours died on the way here or something."

Cara offered a fake smile. "Looks like it," she said, and went up to her room.

"Tell me, what exactly do babysitters do?"

"Make or take us to dinner," Knox told me.

"Let's go out," I suggested. "I don't make dinner. Only smoothies."

"Perfect. I could use a going-out moment tonight any-ways." Knox said this with the slightest sparkle in his eye.

I knew that look: he had a new piece to wear, and tonight would be its inaugural wearing.

Cara, when we coaxed her from her room, was super stoked that my rental was a black Escalade with tints. Almost too stoked. It did, however, feel gratifying to see her smile genuinely for the first time since meeting her. I still thought she was acting like a twat, though. According to some obscure sibling law, it was her night to pick the restaurant, so we went to a place called Ledo Pizza, which sells pizza that's cut in small squares, not slices. Pizza's not chic in the first place, but square pizza? I dreaded the meal from the moment she said the name of the restaurant as we all got in the car, but it was my first night so I wasn't going to get into a fight with her about my dietary restrictions. The point was: we were doing stuff together. Cute.

"Sounds great!" I lied. "You just let me know how to get there. Also, I'm gonna smoke because you guys aren't babies so it's safe." I started the car, backed out of that cozy little driveway, lit a Marlboro Light, and we were off. Babe and her first first cousins.

Ledo's was bright as fuck, Jesus. And I don't mean the lighting, I just mean the color choices. The signage and seating were all red and assaulting to the eyes—sunglasses went on immediately. Once seated—Knox and myself on one side of the table, Cara on the other—a rotund waiter who looked a bit like the clock from *Beauty and the Beast* came over with some menus. Cara immediately pulled out her phone, put headphones in, and started texting or doing Facebook or whatever suburban teens do.

"How y'all doin'? I'm Jimmy, and I'll be servin' you guys tonight."

We all looked at him and smiled.

"Y'all know what y'all wanna drink?" he asked, pulling out his little pad of paper. I'd forgotten about those little pads. In LA waiters memorize your orders because they're used to memorizing lines for auditions they'll never book.

"Coke, please," Cara and Knox responded in unison, not looking up.

"Regular Coke?" I asked them.

"Yep," they said, also together.

This may have been the first time I've seen someone drink a full-strength, full-calorie Coca-Cola.

"Two Cokes, got it. And how 'bout for you, ma'am?"

"I'll have a sparkling water, please."

"Club soda all right?"

"If you must," I conceded.

"Great."

"With lemon."

"You got it. I'll give y'all a minute and be back for your food order."

Jimmy made his way back toward the kitchen. He was wearing orthopedic sneakers of some kind that were almost chic in a normcore way. Wait, I hated normcore. Was this fish so far out of her water that her entire aesthetic eye was being disrupted? Shudder. I shook my head and turned back to Knox, who had started speaking.

"So," he said to me in a hushed tone, "you're gonna have a hard time finding something to eat on this menu."

"I can already tell. Is Cara into playing pranks or something? Because coming here is a sick joke."

"I know," he laughed. "She loves it. I used to beg her and Mom not to make us come here. I'd rather cook for everyone than eat sauce from a can."

"You cook?"

"Food is my passion. Well, good food."

I took a moment to process the maturity level of this miniature person sitting next to me. Was this a Benjamin Button situation? Shouldn't he be into video games and boogers? I had no parameters for child behavior. I didn't know many ten-year-old boys besides Pauly Shore.

"I'd normally guffaw at someone's general 'passion' in food, but I feel like it's super chic for you," I applauded Knox.

Jimmy brought the drinks. There was no lemon in mine. I held in a scream.

"Yeah, it's really my happy place. In the kitchen. *My Father's Daughter* by Gwyneth Paltrow is, like, my favorite book."

Full body chills.

"I know it's a cookbook but I'm serious. The recipes are pretty easy and healthy, too," he continued. "I know you really like her too, right?"

"Yes," I said, nearly brought to tears by the sensation of oneness I was feeling between Knox and me. "Gwyneth is very important to me. She's one of my only role models. Up there with Babe Paley and RuPaul."

"All strong women," Knox agreed, taking his attention back to the menu. "So I suggest you go for the pizza, even though you probably don't eat pizza. Do you?"

"Never."

"I thought so. The salad is not cute, though. They only use romaine at this location, and it's always the white leaves, which you know have little to no nutrients. I just let Cara get the pizza, then I scrape off the cheese and bacon, which she will order, and throw on a little black pepper. Two to three pieces max."

"I'm just gonna order a raw cucumber, some red wine vinegar as a dip," I told him.

"That's actually a brilliant idea. Why have I never thought of that?"

"You're welcome."

"Should we also split a plate of grilled chicken?"

"Sure," I agreed.

This budding friendship was getting so cute I almost Instagrammed a photo of him, but then people would know where I was.

"Y'all ready to order?" Jimmy asked, suddenly standing at the end of our table. The restaurant's carpeted floors made it easy for him to sneak up on us.

"Yep," Cara answered, looking up from her big, weird Android phone in its plastic *Nightmare Before Christmas* case. "We'll have a medium pizza with bacon, super well-done. Thanks."

"Sounds good. Anything else tonight?"

"Absolutely," I assured Jimmy, shocked that he'd expect me to include myself in Cara's downward pizza spiral. "We'll have a plate of grilled chicken, by itself, and a cucumber, peeled."

"Just a cucumber?"

"*Sí.*"

"Y'all sure?"

We'd confused Jimmy.

"One hundred percent. And a ramekin of red wine vinegar, please. Thanks, Jimmy. You're so sweet."

Knox chuckled, probably out of discomfort. Sweet little Knox.

"Well, all right," Jimmy said and made his way to place our order.

I noticed Cara was staring at me like I was an alien. "You guys are so weird."

"Thanks," said Knox.

The food came pretty quickly, which was nice because it meant we could get out of there sooner. I ended up trying the pizza. Knox was right: canned sauce is a soul-crushing experience. I swore then that the next time I went to Italy, I'd take Knox.

FOUR

Getting Over the Death of Lauren Bacall.

We got back to the house after pizza night and right away I noticed that through the windows, the house looked smoky inside. We went in through the garage and a smoke alarm was going off like a wild banshee. I rushed into the kitchen and saw a huge blaze coming from the oven. For some reason, I was compelled to walk toward the flames. I could see that there was actually something on fire inside the oven, which I now noticed was open.

What was most strange was that my best friends Genevieve and Roman were sitting at the kitchen table with

Jimmy the waiter, and they were eating Ledo pizza and drinking HUGE fucking milk shakes.

"What the fuck, Gen?"

"What the fuck to you, Babe? I can't believe you never introduced me to Jimmy. He's fucking hot, and this pizza is tasty as fuck!" Gen replied and then began making out with Jimmy.

What in the actual fuck is going on right now?

"ROMAN," I shouted, "do you not see this fire? Why are you guys just sitting there?"

"Babe, you need to chill out. You're with your family now. Nothing bad can happen to you because you are a Gemini warrior princess."

None of this was adding up. Why were Gen and Roman at Veronica's house? I started walking toward the fire in the oven. I got close enough to see what was burning in there. It was a small picture frame with a picture of me as a baby in it. Baby Babe was being held by an older man who wasn't my dad. This man was older than my dad would have been when I was born. I didn't recognize the picture, but I recognized that it was me because I distinctly remember seeing other pictures of me as a newborn wearing that same exact hideous onesie. I'd never seen this picture before. Who was this man? He was really handsome.

The picture frame was clearly on fire, but it wasn't burning or turning black. I was genuinely freaked the fuck out. I started screaming at the top of my lungs.

"GET ME THE FUCK OUT OF HERE, PLEASE!!!!"

I felt a hand grab my shoulder firmly and I turned to see who it was.

That must have been when I woke up. I realized at that moment that I was back in bed, in the guest room at Veronica's house. I was still screaming, but now I was screaming directly into the face of a woman I'd never seen in my life.

"BABE!"

"Who are you?" I said, trying to calm myself down. She was tall and thin and had a kind face. She looked concerned.

"I'm Vee. Veronica. I'm Knox and Cara's mom."

"You're my aunt."

"That's right."

"So you're Donna's sister?"

"Unfortunately."

I loved that she was immediately down to shit on my mom/her sister within twelve seconds of meeting me. The public and general agreement that Donna was a huge disappointment when it came to all things family comforted me. I'm not the only one she fucked over. I liked that Veronica shared that with me straightaway. First impressions are everything.

"Where is that bitch?" I asked.

Then last night came back to me. In true Donna fashion, she wasn't at the house when we'd returned from dinner. I'd waited up for her to arrive, but she never showed so I just went to bed at, like, 1 a.m. If nothing else, at least my mother is fucking consistent in her unflinching disregard for everyone but herself. I mean, narcissism can be chic, just not when it's your mom.

"Who knows where Donna ever is? She isn't picking up her phone, but I can see that her texts are being read, so . . ."

"I'm Babe."

"I know."

I extended my hand out toward Veronica. It was really awkward. What is the protocol for when you meet your only aunt after twenty-seven years? She looked at me confused/ sad or something. Then she just hugged as hard as she could. She was squeezing me so tightly. I honestly couldn't breathe.

"I've never missed anyone I didn't actually know. But I just realized that I've missed you, Babe," Veronica said quietly as she continued suffocating me. She was really strong.

I didn't know what to say.

"I can be a real cunt," I offered. "So maybe the idea of me is better than actually knowing me."

"I doubt it. I feel bad that I didn't make more of an effort to reach out to you once Donna reconnected with you."

"You shouldn't. I didn't know you existed until Donna told me about you, like, five days ago. Family is weird."

"Your, well, our family is very weird, and you're going to be meeting a lot of them today at the party."

Oh shit. The party. Between all the pizza and travel and nightmares and the fact that I was still getting over the death of Lauren Bacall, I'd forgotten about the reason I'd come to this strange land. My grandfather was turning eighty or something. Just the fact that I have a grandfather was pretty strange and hard for me to wrap my head around. I'd only ever known my grandmother, Tai Tai. She was the only grandparent I thought I'd ever know. But I guess I was going to meet my mother's father today.

"What's this party going to be like? Where is it? What am I wearing? I randomly packed a lot of Gucci but I think that'll be too floral if the event is outside. Give me some guidance, I feel lost."

"The party's here. At the house. In the backyard. You've been sleeping almost the whole day so the guests should start arriving in about an hour."

"Fuck. An hour?"

"Yeah. So I'll leave you to get ready."

"Okay. An hour's not gonna be enough time, but okay. I'll rush. Thanks, Veronica."

She smiled and turned to walk out of the room.

"Hey, Vee." I stopped her just before she slipped away. "Really, what are you going to wear to this party? Is it casual cocktail? A little more formal? Could use some guidance on the general vibes. This is my first time visiting this geographical region of the United States."

"Well, I'm already dressed for the occasion, so perhaps this will give you some sense."

"That's hilarious. You're funny. I guess funny runs in the family because I'm one of the funniest people I know."

"I'm not kidding, Babe."

DEAD SILENCE.

During this awkward moment I stared at the whole picture. She was wearing what can only be described as a pink satin pajama top and stretchy, yoga-y cargo pants. Maybe that's really hard to imagine, but trust me when I tell you that she was definitely wearing them and they were definitely an assault on the eyes.

On the other hand, I noticed that she had incredible bone structure and, from what I could tell, underneath her blousy abomination it looked like she kept things pretty tight and fit. Donna has a great body, but she's a model who hasn't eaten a solid food in three decades. Way to go, Mom. But clearly there was a genetic component to her body story, because suburban-Sally Veronica over here was also giving me very good body vibes.

"I'm gonna go change now," Veronica said quietly, almost to herself.

"Sounds good. Me too."

I showered, blew my hair dry, lotioned up, meditated, chanted, returned some pressing emails, stretched, and then put on my black Erdem lace dress and headed downstairs. The party was in full swing at that point as I had taken (oops) two hours to get ready. Their bathroom was economy-sized. I also noted that people in Maryland arrive to parties when they start, unlike in New York and Los Angeles, where people get there when the party is ending. The people at the party all looked very Maryland-esque, if I'm being honest. The scene: ill-fitting jeans, taupe turtlenecks but not in a Kim K. way, jewelry from Zales, Sperry Top-Siders, Abercrombie skirts, chain bracelets, general basicness. But, the backyard was actually decorated beautifully. Someone with a good eye for design had put some serious thought into this shit. There were supple bouquets of gerbera daisies hanging in explosive bundles from the trees, and the party's planner—whoever she was—had mastered the space with a simple and functional table layout. Basically, it was way chicer than it needed to be, which I always appreciate.

"What do you think of my work?" I heard a small voice say.

It was Knox.

"You did all this?"

"Well, your mom paid for the decorations, because my mom has no artistic vision slash is very, very stingy with money. But I made all aesthetic choices and I also made the hors d'oeuvres."

Knox was wearing an all-black sweatsuit that was either Yeezy for Adidas or just some ordinary sweats that he'd bought at a mall and then intentionally destroyed enough to make them look expensive as fuck. Either way it was fucking fabulous, and I was living for it. His hair was slicked back and gelled. He looked ummmmmmazing. I was overcome by an emotion with which I don't have that much experience: pride. I mean, I've been proud of myself many times, and I'm proud of my friends when they do something incredible, like get a promotion at work or settle out of court when they're trying to sue their parents for more inheritance. But that inevitably comes with the accompanying emotion: jealousy. This was different. I was just proud of him. I wanted the best for him. He was clearly very talented and he was clearly very much my relative, and for that he should enjoy all the happiness in the world.

"I think it looks perfect out here. I couldn't have done it better myself."

"Really?"

"Yeah, really."

"Wow. Babe Walker likes my party planning. Okay. Let me just digest that. I need to run into the kitchen to check on my gluten-free option. It's almost ready to be plated."

"What is it?"

"Salmon sashimi lettuce cup with tamari dipping sauce. And yes, it's low-sodium tamari."

"Love."

He disappeared, and I walked to a small table in the corner where the alcohol was. I poured myself a glass of rosé (very thoughtful of Knox to have made sure they had my drink), downed it quickly, and poured myself a second. No one, and I mean no one, at this party was looking at me. It was just a weird feeling, so I thought I would mention it.

Then I saw something that freaked me out: a man on the other side of the yard who was sitting by himself. It was the man from the picture in the dream I'd had last night. It was him. At least, it looked a lot like him.

"Who are you?" I asked as I walked up to him.

"I'm Joe."

Joe was wearing a simple washed-out blue oxford and khakis. He was handsome in a Kurt Russell way but older, much older. It hit me that this man was probably my grandfather. If it makes you uncomfortable that I just called my own maybe-grandfather handsome, then please remind yourself that I'd never met/seen/heard anything about this man until this very moment. He was a completely stranger. Relax. And BTW, ew. I would never. I'm not Genevieve.

"Who are you?" he asked.

"I'm Donna's daughter. Babe. Babe Walker."

He looked at me.

"I see. Of course you are. Well, in that case, it's nice to see you again."

"Well, we've never met before, Joe. I've never been here before."

"I know that. But we met in California. When you were born."

"We did?" I was kinda creeped out at this point.

"Of course we did. You think I would miss the birth of my first grandchild?"

"Oh. Wow. You're my grandfather."

"Yup."

"That makes a lot of sense. I need a drink."

"Me too."

"Happy birthday?"

"Thanks. Mind getting me a drink?"

I went and got us a bottle of tequila (Joe's signature

drink, apparently) and we sat together and got acquainted. He was tall, handsome, and so calm. I mean, yes, we were there celebrating his eightieth year so I wasn't expecting him to be jumping around, but his energy was gentle and strong. I liked being around him. Had I seen that picture of Joe and me somewhere? I must have. Maybe at Tai Tai's?

"So where is your mother?" Joe asked, sipping on a shot of tequila.

"I was wondering the same thing. But really I think a better question to ask is, where is your daughter?"

"That's true, but I learned a long time ago that Donna does what Donna wants to do. Always has, always will."

"That took me about twenty-six years to figure out. Actually, I think I'm still figuring it out."

"Look, dear. You really got a raw deal. Your mother is really no mother at all."

"It's fine, Joe. I fuckin' get that. She wasn't there for me my whole life, but I'm still here and I'm gonna prove to everyone that my life does have purpose, and that family does mean something to me."

"She hasn't been there for either of you kids."

"Well, it's just me," I reminded him. I guess he was just the teensiest bit senile. That's fine.

"Not exactly." Joe lowered his voice to a whisper.

"What do you mean?" I perked up.

"Oh, I don't mean anything by it, darlin'. When she was young, I thought Donna would grow out of her selfishness and become a little more of a responsible, caring individual, ya know what I mean? But there is only so much that you can do to shape a child. You do your best. You put in the work. Veronica over here turned out to be the good egg. A really good egg. She's my shining star. She is one of the most hardworking, thoughtful women I know. And I tell her every chance I get."

"Yeah. She seems really nice. And very different from Donna."

"You have no idea how different she really is from Donna. She's been cleaning up every mess Donna makes since they were little girls."

Joe was slurring his words, slightly, at this point. He'd had at least five shots of tequila, which I think is way more than five in old-people years. But I wasn't quite sure what he was getting at.

"Well, I'm glad I came, even if my deadbeat mom never shows up. It's nice to meet this side of the family. Knox is adorable."

"You think so, huh? Yeah, he's a pretty amazing kid. Makes a great steak."

"I'm sure he does. Seems like he's very talented in the culinary arts."

"Fucking Donna. Couldn't even show up for her old man's eightieth. I mean, that I can live with. It's that she missed all of Knox's cooking and planning that makes me angry."

"Are they close?"

"No. I wouldn't say that. Donna's never around enough to be close to any of us. But I think she's done a marginally better job with Knox than she did with you."

"Exsqueeze me, what are you talking about?"

"Knox isn't your cousin, darlin'."

Just at that moment, Cara, Knox, and Veronica burst raucously out of the house carrying a birthday cake, singing "Happy Birthday." But I couldn't escape the moment Joe and I were having. I was in shock. Was this man, my grandfather, who I just met an hour ago, trying to tell me that Knox was Donna's kid? Did I have a fucking brother? I mouthed the words to the fucking song like a robot, eyes glazed, took a few swigs of tequila, and walked up into the house. I hated Donna more and more by the minute, and it seemed like almost everyone else in this family did, too.

How could she have not shown up to this? I was drunk, tired, and sad. I never went back down to the party. I just got into bed, watched *Transparent* on my iPad, and fell asleep.

About four hours later at 3 a.m. I was awake again. My phone was buzzing. It was a text from Donna.

Donna Turn the light on. I'm in this room with you right now

Babe What are you talking about?

Donna Vee says we should share this bed

I looked up and there she was standing by the door. What a fucking psycho.

FIVE

Hushed, Aggressive, Chic, Threatening, and Scared.

Ugh. Okay. I was going to have to deal with this if I wanted to get any sleep, which I did.

"This is some kind of sick joke she's playing on us, right?"

"I don't fucking know, Babe," Donna said, dumping her oxblood overstuffed Balenciaga Papier tote onto the floor.

I was suddenly sure Veronica was mad at me for coming and mad at my mom for being a cunt for basically her entire life, and now we were being punished by having to share a room with each other. I hadn't shared a room with someone I wasn't fucking, even on vacation, in thirty years, and I'm not even thirty yet.

"Veronica must be mad at us," I suggested. "But we both know sharing a room isn't gonna work . . . for me."

"I know."

"And when things don't work for me, they tend to not work for the people around me."

"I know, Babe. We've met," Donna said, the last part sliding out slightly under her breath, which I could tell smelled like an American Spirit Blue—that's what my mom smoked. I'll never understand those cigarettes. They take twice as long to smoke as Marlboro Lights and honestly who has the time? Not to mention the fact that they're adorned with Native American–themed art, which just isn't nearly agreeable enough an aesthetic to accessorize with *every single d*—

"I'll go talk to her," Donna said, cutting off my train of thought.

"Do what you want. But please figure it out."

She held her look at me; it was a loaded stare.

"Are you trying to tell me something with your eyes?"

"I'm just exhausted, Babe. My flight from Idaho was two hours delayed, they ran out of red wine literally halfway over Colorado, and I forgot to pack Xanax, which meant I sat up sober and miserable for the next four hours of the flight."

"Idaho?" I inquired.

"Sun Valley. Friend's house out there. Gay wedding."

"Chic."

"I'm gonna go deal with this. I'll stay at a hotel if I need to."

"Yes, thank you," I said, pulling the sheets back over my head.

The blinds in that bedroom were literally useless. They were beige with the weight of a thin crepe—I didn't even understand the point of having them there hanging from the top of the windows. In my opinion, blackout curtains are the only option. Otherwise, just sleep outside and be an animal. I should've taken a pill like I had the night before. That was clearly the only way to get any sleep around here. So I was up at 6 or 9 a.m. or something heinous like that. I rolled myself out of bed, threw on a floor-length cashmere cape (black of course), covered my face in an awakening raw coconut, raw cocaine, raw pear mask, and made my way down to the house's public quarters. Luckily, no one was up so the living room/kitchen area (it was one room . . . not clear) was empty. I made myself a cup of tea, and by tea I mean hot water and lemon, and went out to the porch with my breakfast, and by breakfast I mean a Marlboro Light.

The air smelled completely different in Maryland. In LA, our air smells like old gasoline cooking on hot rocks with a slight splash of Chloé Eau de Parfum; here the breeze pas

de bourrée'd across my face smelling like trees. I have to say
I didn't hate the feeling it gave me. I didn't hate it at all. I
wouldn't even be lying if I told you that in that *very* brief
moment, I was happy to be in Shithole, MD. I lit my cigarette and closed my eyes for a moment.

"You can't smoke out here."

It was Cara.

"I'll wait for your mom to tell me that. It's her house." I
sucked in another drag. "I'm not sure if you realize this, but
you're ten years old," I said without turning to face her. She
was deliberately fucking up my moment, so she deserved
nothing more than my back.

"I'm fourteen," Cara bit back.

"Whatever, you know what I mean."

"Knox is ten."

"Cute."

"And my mom *will* tell you to stop smoking on her property," Cara assured me.

"Is your mom out here?"

"I'll wake her up."

I spun around quickly and looked right at her. I shit you
not, she was wearing a Snuggie.

"You would never."

"You're right, I wouldn't. I'm not a fuckin' snitch," Cara
said.

I couldn't help but laugh. She said it with such conviction, I thought I was watching *Mob Wives* or some other ratchet television program.

"So can I have a drag?" she asked, stepping toward me.

"Really?"

"Yeah. I started smoking two months ago. My mom doesn't know, so obviously don't tell her."

"Hmmmmm," I shrugged. Maybe I had more in common with this little bitch than I had first thought. "Sure," I said, "get over here."

I held out my cigarette to the minor standing before me, and she took a long, professional drag. I wondered if Cara had given a blow job yet, and what about penis-in-vagina sex? I have a strict no-children-around-me rule so I didn't really have anyone to compare her to, but she certainly seemed to be very adult for fourteen years old. Cara handed the cigarette back to me, I took a last drag, and threw the butt underneath the porch.

"Thanks, Babe," she said before turning quickly and running back into the house, presumably to wash the cigarette smell off her hands. Before she made it to the screen door, I called out—

"Don't wear Snuggies anymore."

I walked down to the yard but was reminded on contact that I loathe the feeling of wet grass between my toes, so I gasped and ran back up and into the house.

It was still so quiet in there. I could hear the faint tumble of Cara shuffling around in the upstairs bathroom, which reminded me of the first time that my dad caught me smoking. I was at my Tai Tai's house, and she'd given me a casual smoke to accompany our cucumber water and sunbathing on a Saturday afternoon. He picked me up earlier than planned and caught me in the back garden wearing a pair of Tai Tai's XL Balenciaga sunglasses and puffing away on a powder-blue Nat Sherman cigarette. The drama of it all must've been too much for my poor dad to handle. He was furious, which I didn't understand at the time because he smokes cigars and weed. It all felt a bit hypocritical. Of course I had to get caught my very first time at the rodeo. That is just so typically me. Looking back, though, I guess it was pretty crazy of my Tai Tai to give a cigarette to a seven-year-old.

I helped myself to some of the almond milk that Knox had made for his party cookies from the fridge. He'd added a dash of cinnamon. Genius.

On the counter was a stack of magazines, every one of them a *Martha Stewart Living*. I sat down to leaf through one because I was that bored. Donna entered the kitchen. White tank top, yoga pants, barefoot, no pedicure.

"Morning, Babe," she said in an almost chipper voice.

"So you figured out another place to sleep, I'm guessing? Or did you just say fuck sleep and take an Adderall?"

"The Adderall wouldn't have been such a bad idea, but unfortunately I ran out last week," Donna said with a chummy laugh that made me feel weird.

She poured a cup of coffee out of a little machine called a Mr. Coffee and sat down next to me.

"No, Vee said I could sleep with her in her bed. It was actually nice. We used to share a bed when we were kids."

"You're kidding."

"Oh, I am so serious," she assured me with a sarcastic but happy smirk.

Hearing about her childhood was odd because I didn't *really* know the first thing about this stranger whose body I happened to grow inside of. Ew.

"Where did you guys live again?" I asked her.

"Well, I was born in Ohio. But when my mom died, Joe moved us here to Maryland where the rest of our family was. Not that far from here, actually. Which, as you know now, gave me plenty of reasons to run away."

"Well, you for sure did that."

"I was never good at logical. My sister was. She was totally fine staying and accepting the tiny scale of her life here." She took a long sip of coffee. "But every time I come back, I'm reminded that she fucking likes it here. Veronica's happy, you know? I don't get it. She's constantly running from a shift at work to a shift at her other work to a thing for Knox or Cara. It must be exhausting. From the looks of her life, you'd think she'd be miserable, but she's happy."

"And from the looks of *your* life one might think you're thriving but really you're miserable?"

Donna cocked her head a bit and just looked at me.

"Don't be a bitch," she said.

"I really don't mean to be a bitch, but honestly, Donna, what you just said was sooooo bitchy."

"What did I say?"

"You're basically saying that Veronica's life sucks but it's nice that she can enjoy it," I told her, almost surprised that I was sticking up for Vee's boring and generally horrible life. Donna looked guilty.

"I so didn't mean it that way. I'm just saying I'm proud of her for making this work for her and her family. They struggle, you know? And she just keeps rolling along. I don't have that stick-to-itiveness in me. I don't think you do either."

"Excuse me?"

"I'm just saying—"

"Now *I'm* being attacked?"

"Hey, no one is being attacked here, Babe. I was just saying—"

"I know about Knox!" I blurted. Donna's eyes squinted as if to say, *Are you sure you want to go there?*

"What are you talking about?" she asked calmly.

"He's exactly like me and nothing like his mother. He even looks like me, and we have the same fear of white carbs."

"Babe, what are you insinuating here?"

"So you're admitting there's something to insinuate?"

"I have no idea what you're talking about."

"Oh, please, Donna," I said and got up. I walked out to the deck—I didn't want Knox walking in and hearing this—and Donna followed me. I live for a dramatic kitchen scene, but if what I thought was true was actually true, finding out like this could fuck him up for sure.

"You gave birth to Knox and left him for Veronica to take care of just like you left me for Dad to take care of," I said in a hushed-but-aggressive-but-chic-but-threatening-but-scared tone.

"Are you insane?"

"Nope."

"Are you completely fucking insane?"

"Still no."

Donna threw her arms up and started to walk away from me.

"Wait," I whisper-yelled. "Can we just talk about this without you acting like a complete fucking baby?"

"Babe. There is nothing to talk about."

"Then how can you explain the similarities? He even looks like me!"

"He does not. Relax."

"He does! And all the shit your dad said to me yesterday. I'm just saying it's a lot and it hit me like a ton of coke bricks last night. The truth will be set free whether you like it or not!"

"Can you not shout?" Donna asked, in a mommish way. I wanted to slap her, but it was too early.

"Yeah, okay, sorry for raising my voice. This is so fucked, though, if it's true, and I totally think it is. Why should I trust you?" I pleaded.

"Fine. That's fair. I've given you plenty of reasons to be skeptical of the life choices I make, but I promise you, Babe, Knox is Vee's kid, and we need to end this conversation now."

Her voice became so stern and serious by the end of the sentence that I knew I'd gone too far. I'd struck a nerve, and when people's nerves are struck, they can turn crazy. I'd learned that in rehab when I wrongly accused this short girl of stealing a *Vanity Fair* from the drawer in my desk. I was super wrong and she got super mad and she super tried to cut my hair off in the middle of the night and I super woke up and with feline grace and force tackled her to the ground and super by accident broke her collarbone. Not my fault, but still, not a cute moment.

ANYWAY. Donna, Knox, me, life.

"I'm gonna go take a shower," she said, heading back inside.

I didn't say anything else to Donna that morning because I felt I'd said enough. I was basically positive that my grandfather was telling me the truth about Knox but I couldn't push it any more. I just had to let it sit inside me and rot away my insides like a cancer. A truth-cancer.

After a few minutes of stillness, I dragged my caped body back into the bright-as-fuck guest room, pulled the covers over my head, and reached for the pill bottle in my Proenza bag on the floor. I knocked back a couple Ambiens and hummed the melody to Lou Reed's "Perfect Day" until I felt Namaste.

For being such a dead zone, Maryland was turning out to be surprisingly stressful.

Before falling asleep, I texted Gen and Roman.

Babe Why have neither of you texted me to see if I'm alive or dead?

Gen Obvs we would have heard if you died.

Babe How would you have heard?

Gen Like on the news or some shit. Or Mabinty would've texted.

Babe You think it'll be on the news when I die?

Gen Maybe

Babe So you don't think that?

Gen It's poss

Babe Roman what do you think?

Babe Roman?

Babe Romie.

Babe Romanowsky

Babe Rebecca Roman Stamos

Gen I think he's at Pilates

Babe So? He keeps his phone on always.

Babe Whatever.

Babe Thanks for thinking it'll be on the news when I die. I mean, I think you're right. A lot of people are going to be sad/ shocked when I die. But that's actually really sweet of you to acknowledge, Genevieve

Babe SO do you wanna know what I'm doing/where I am/ what I'm wearing or what?

Gen Not really

Babe K then tell me what you're doing

Gen I'm texting with you

Babe Cute. Where?

Gen This dude's house

Babe Oh yeah, it's early there. What dude??

Babe And since when did we say dude?

Gen I know, that was horrible, no idea why I said that. This GUY. This GUYs house

Babe Yeah that feels so much better

Babe What guy?

Gen Honestly, I can't remember his name but his house is the absolute shit. So happy I woke up here. I guess he went to work? I haven't looked around for a note or anything but he's definitely not in this bedroom. Or at least I think he's not.

Babe Tell me everything

Gen Honestly it's not even a fun hookup story

Babe I don't give a shit. Dish. Now. I'm so bored.

Gen Fine.

Gen I was at Sunset Tower last night with Lauren and Lauren and we ran into these guys who knew them so we all started dancing and I ended up drinking some molly water and making out with this guy's ear for literally forty-five minutes, which sounds insane but it was sexy and he just wasn't stopping me and you know how I can go off on someone's ear if they don't pull away

Babe I hate that you like doing that

Gen I hate it too, but it's who I am and I can't change that

Babe And I respect that. I hate it but I respect it

Gen Thanks

Babe So how did you end up in this strange and sexy bed?

Gen After the club, I decided it's a good idea to get into this guy's Ferrari with him. He's wasted btw

Babe Gen

Gen I know. So he really wanted road head and he was hot enough so I obliged

Babe Pic for proof

Gen I don't have one. But if you Google 'Marc Saudi Arabia Tiger Rescue' he should be like the first pic that comes up

Babe Just did

Babe Hot

Gen Right?

Babe I mean, love that for you. Not for me.

Gen No trust me you'd wanna fuck him Babe

Babe Trust me I wouldn't

Gen Trust me you would

Babe Trust me. I would not.

Gen No but like you would. Trust me.

Babe I think I like definitely, one million percent, would never fuck that guy, even if someone was holding a gun to my head. But LOVE him for you!

Gen Anyway

Gen He was really funny and had soft ear skin AND he told me that he had a tiger sanctuary in his backyard

Babe And?

Gen Yes! And you know how much I love wild cats. His house is a literal castle. There are three Damien Hirsts in the kitchen. There's a woman dressed as a mermaid who swims in his pool every day from 5pm to 5am. Could you die?

Babe I'll pass, but you do love a wild cat moment. I always thought that was a pinch too Kardashian of you but I'm not here to judge

Gen Think what you will

Babe You know I always do

Gen His cats are amazing. We went in and played with them which is so fun on molly and really the whole night ended up being lovely. There were some other people that came over and I swear one of them was Jaden Smith. AND he gave me these huge diamond studs that he said he was gonna give to some other girl. Such a sweetheart. But I don't exactly remember having sex with him and I am in his bed and he is not which weirds me out just a tiny bit.

Babe I think you should grab your shit, call an uber, and pump the fuck out of there

Gen Yeah, I'm totally gonna do that. After I shower. I smell like a pet store from the tigers.

Babe Just vomited

Babe Love you

Gen Love you. Have fun.

Babe You don't even know where I am

Gen Oh yeah, where are you?

Babe Donna invited me to her dad's 80th birthday party so I came to Maryland and I'm meeting like all of these family people that I didn't even know existed

Gen Weird

Babe You have no idea. Stay tuned for updates

Gen K

Babe Get out of that zoo

Gen K

Roman Hey binches! What I miss.

Babe Nothing I gotta go sleep. It's nap time here.

Roman Where?

Babe Night my queens

Gen Later slut

Roman Fine. Bye. Genevieve call me

SIX

Fuck Babies.

I woke up a little bit later. Six p.m.

Fabulous, I thought, one more day down basically. Existence in Maryland, albeit temporary, may not have been as hellish as I'd imagined it to be, but I wasn't trying to sow seeds for a new life and grow roots there. So I figured I'd stay for two more days. I'd smoke a few more cigarettes with underage Cara, find new ways to be passive-aggressive toward my mom, and get to know sweet angel Knox a little bit better. I even mulled over the possibility of burning that carpeted pizza place down, stealing Knox, and taking him to LA to be my assistant/cousin/son/protégé.

"What's the possibility of getting a good massage in this town in the next thirty minutes?" I asked as I emerged from the bedroom and into the living room. It was empty.

"Hello?"

Was the whole house empty?

"HELLO?" I said louder. "It's me, Babe. Is anyone home?"

"In here," I heard Knox's voice say from the kitchen.

The kitchen was cluttered with cooking supplies and food things but there was no one else around besides the little chef, smock and everything. Is it called a smock? Apron? Chef's robe? I can never remember the names of tools. Anyway, he was standing on a footstool at the edge of the counter, his little head almost buried in a large metal mixing bowl. "Hey, Babe," he said.

"Making dinner?" I asked.

"Yep, hope you like lasagna!"

My heart sank to the ugly tile floor and shattered. How would I tell him that I don't eat cheese or pasta or regular-sodium tomato sauce? From the looks of the room, he'd been prepping this meal all day.

His little head popped up from behind the bowl. There was a smear of tomato across his cheek. "It's vegan and raw."

"Oh my God," I blurted, "you scared the actual fuck out of me!"

"I figured," he said with an adorbs laugh, emptying the contents of the bowl into a large baking dish, which was almost already filled. "No, no, no. No way I'd make a conventional lasagna in this house. That's, like, so boring."

"And just, like . . . "

"Unhealthy," he said for the both of us.

"Exactly."

I grabbed a glass of unsweetened mint tea from the fridge and took a seat on one of the stools at the counter. I watched Knox in his element. He used the flat side of a large spoon (ladle? lasso?) to smooth what looked like a semichunky tomato, basil, and yellow-pepper salsa over the top of the lasagna and did so with such grace and command that it almost made me weep into my iced tea. I once had a boyfriend that could cook, like, super well or whatever and everyone was always screaming and losing their shit about how "amazing and oh my Gooodddd so simple!" his food was, but he was a full-grown adult so I wasn't impressed. But *this* was like watching a baby breakdance or a dog skateboard. It made zero sense, it was a little strange, but it was beautiful and life-affirming nonetheless.

He put a sheet of parchment paper over the lasagna and slid it to the side.

"How are you five years old?"

"I'm ten," Knox said seriously.

"Whatever. That's what I meant."

"I don't know. Cooking just comes naturally to me. My mom always says 'be natural.'" *That could be a good mantra*, I thought. He threw a dishrag over one shoulder, kicked his footstool over to the sink, and started to wash his hands with his back toward me. "Like style does for you."

"That's maybe one of the sweetest things anyone's ever said to me probably."

"I loved reading your books. I already told you that, I think, right? I read them two summers ago. Both of them—one right after the other. My mom said they were too adult for me, but I told her that was bullshit and she took them away so I had to buy them on iBooks and read them on my iPod touch."

"Wait," I stopped him, "what's an iPod touch?"

"It's like an iPhone but without the phone part."

"Got it."

"So anyway, I had to find a way to finish the second book because I really wanted to know what happened with Robert and—"

Donna, Veronica, and Cara walked into the kitchen, and Knox stopped talking. He just finished washing a few things, wiped down the sink, and came to sit next to me at the counter.

"Hey, guys," I offered. None of them looked at me. Cara was wearing something yellow and fleece. Donna came over and put her hand on my shoulder. Through the sheer Prada tank dress I was wearing, her fingers felt long and thin and cold and pointedly chic.

"You sleep all right?" she asked in a condescending tone. Why was she being weird to me now? Did I hit a nerve before with the maternity thing? Was she threatened by my investigative prowess? Having Veronica around must've been stressing her out.

"Yep!" I gloated. "I needed that! Lot on my mind lately and my psyche was like, 'Whoa, you need to sleep!' So I'm glad I slept all day. What did you ladies do? Go to Barneys? Just kidding."

"We had a great day, beautiful spring day out there. Some fresh air might do you good, Babe," answered Veronica.

"Was that a hint of shade I just detected in your voice, Veronica?"

But without acknowledging me, she just kept on, "We ready for dinner, Knoxers?"

"Yep," he said, hopping down from the stool. "Let me just grab the salad out of the fridge and I'll take it out to the table. You guys go ahead and sit." He was so cute.

The shit my grandfather had said was still eating away at me. I felt phony as fuck. It just wasn't like me to pretend like things are cool when they're simply fucking not. As we walked over to eat, a lump grew in my throat. Like I knew I was going to say something about it that I shouldn't even be thinking. Like when you're already paying for three Dior skirts and out of the corner of your eye you see a gorgeous, supple camel Loewe bucket tote, and you know you're going to run over and add it to your tab. But you shouldn't buy it. You don't even like bucket bags. You don't want it. But you need it so fucking bad it hurts.

They had a small dining room with a six-person table next to the kitchen. Knox had set the fuck out of that table. It was basic because he didn't have much to work with, but the ideas were strong. He'd put a tiny bundle of fresh-cut flowers on each of our plates and the placemats were laminated collages of fashion magazine cutouts from the 1970s and '80s. I was excited to move food around on top of Candice Bergen's face.

We sat at our designated seats; Knox had made place cards, obviously. His calligraphy could use some work. I was at the head of the table, which, to be honest, made me feel a little awkward. I deserved the esteemed position because I'd traveled the farthest and probably dealt with the most hardship in my life of anyone there, but I could tell that the rest of the women in my "family" were annoyed that Knox was giving me spesh treatment.

"This looks delicious!" Donna said as the raw lasagna was placed on the table next to a colorful salad and a

large bowl of fresh cashew pesto tossed with raw zuc-
chini angel hair. It really did look like some shit I would
eat at home at Café Gratitude, one of my favorite Larch-
mont haunts. This little boy just understood me. They all
started to dig in. I decided to refrain until the vulturing
had stopped.

"This is a really awesome dinner, Knox. Is this from your
show?" Cara said through a mouthful of lasagna.

"What show?" I asked.

"*MasterChef Junior*. A reality cooking competition for
kids. It's on Fox. I really want to be on it. And NO, Cara,
this is my own original recipe. I don't learn recipes on that
show, I'm not a copycat."

"Can we please not talk about this again?" Veronica
interjected, loudly. "You are not going on that show. Is it
possible to get through one meal without talking about that
damn show?"

"Yes, Mom. It's completely possible to not talk about
MasterChef Junior. As long as you're willing to accept that
you are crushing my dreams and hopes."

Awkwardness.com

"So . . ." I said, breaking the dull hum of chewing sounds.
"I slept, Knox cooked, what did *you* guys do today?"

"Tried to kill myself twenty different ways," Cara kindly
shared.

"Cara, please," said an annoyed but totally deadpan Veronica.

"What. It's true. You know I can't stand that girl."

Veronica put her fork down and took a sip of the beer she was drinking (out of a can . . . ?). "Cara had her physics tutor today because Rebecca, the tutor, wasn't able to do their regular Wednesday meeting this week."

"Sucks," I said.

"I shouldn't have to go to her on the weekend. It's cruel and unusual."

"Point taken, Cara. Get over it now. You can't get another D this term so we gotta do what we gotta do, okay?"

"You actually *can* get Ds and be totally fine," I assured her. *Maybe that's my mantra?*

"Babe." Veronica and Donna said at the same time with scolding looks. Cara and Knox both lit up.

"Okay, okay. Just kidding. Listen to your mom or whatever. Always listen to your mom."

"Babe, can you pass the salt?" Veronica asked me.

"Sure." I said with a smile as I passed it to her with the pepper—you always pass the two as a pair; my Tai Tai once slapped me for passing the salt alone. "See, I never had a mom to listen to." I then said with a glance to Donna who was strategically not looking at me, "I had a dad, though, he was fabulous, still is. One day you'll meet him."

No one uttered a word. I still hadn't taken any food, which I guess was rude of me judging by the look on Veronica's face, so I scooped some rawsagna onto my plate and moved it around. What was her damage?

"Anyways, so isn't it weird that you guys are so different? Like, Veronica, you're basically the opposite of Donna. I mean, you look like her as fuck, but your—"

"Language, please," Veronica said.

"Sorry, AF. But your lives are so completely opposite of each other's. Donna is never in one place, never sleeping with the same person, never addicted to the same drug, and you're, like, super normal." They both seemed a little disturbed by my statement, but I cared zero much. It was the truth! It's not my fault that Donna was a huge mess of a nonmother. An absentee mom, if you will. "And Knox is the opposite of Cara," I continued. "No? It's almost as if they have different parents or at least different moms or something. Like, Knox is so me and Cara is so not. Don't get me wrong, Cara, you're very interesting and, like, totally a real American teenager and that has its merits, but it's just so not me."

The table seemed to be looking anywhere but at me. Donna just shook her head as if I was an embarrassment. Whatever, Donna.

Hey, I was feeling this way so I just put it out all there. Fuck it. Not to mention, I was a little bit *boo whore* about

Veronica ignoring me before dinner and then telling me to alter *my* speech. I don't alter my speech. That's just not a thing that I do or am told to do. I say what I mean, *Veronica*. Did she not know I was a writer? Words are, like, my thing.

"Knox," Donna said, "I feel like you're tall for your age. Are you taller than the kids in your grade?"

"Being tall is chic," I told him, but he wasn't tall.

Knox smiled at me. "I guess I'm kind of tall? The other boys in my grade are pretty big. They all play sports and so they're definitely bigger than me."

"Are there bullies in your school?" I asked, concerned.

"No," Veronica interjected. "There aren't bullies, right, Knoxie?"

Knoxie? . . . Cringe.

He forced a grin. "No, Mom. Not really. They're pretty strict about it now."

"What would they have to bully you about anyway?"

What? Was she blind? Veronica seemed oblivious to the fact that living under her very own roof was a delicate flower of a boy whose interests were fashion, health, and Babe Walker. I mean, this boy was clearly a gay princess goddess angel from heaven and EXACTLY the type of fragile flora that idiot grade-school boys like to prey on. I didn't say anything.

"That's right," I said. "You can take care of yourself."

"I think so. And when anyone messes with me, I just have Cara deal with it."

Cara smiled.

"What is that supposed to mean?" Veronica asked.

"Nothing," Knox said. "Nothing. I'm fine, Mom."

"Do you need me to talk with one of your teachers, Knox? I'm going to see them in a couple of days at Back to School Night."

"Really, Mom. I'm fine."

It was getting a little tense, so I took a bite of the food. It was delicious. I felt another wave of pride and awe wash over me. I never let food get involved in my emotional being but I truly couldn't help it this time—Knox's lasagna was just that good.

Veronica and Donna started having their own conversation, something about my grandfather's house, which left my end of the table to talk to each other, or not.

"Were you always tall?" I asked Knox.

"Yeah, my mom said I was a big baby, but to be honest, Babe, I don't really like talking about when I was a baby."

"Oh, okay."

"Yeah, babies are just kinda gross to me."

"Same," Cara agreed.

"Great, fine, totally get it. Not gonna talk about babies. Fuck babies."

"Hey, maybe tomorrow after school, do you think we could go through my closet and do a heavy edit?" Knox asked me.

"Are you kidding?"

"Um, no. Is that rude to assume you'd wanna do that?"

"Sounds like a fucking nightmare," Cara muttered.

"I would honestly like nothing more!" I shouted. "I live for the fact that you live for fashion. How did that even happen?"

"The Internet, duh," he said.

"Right, duh."

Cara was Snapchatting herself pretending to vomit the lasagna. It was horrifying to see.

"So you just watch the shows in Paris, New York, et cetera, from your computer? That's so unchic slash chic! I commend you. Living in the woods and still devoting yourself to style like that."

"We don't really live in the woods."

"But, like . . ."

"Okay, fine. We live in the middle of the woods."

"And you eat at carpeted pizza places."

"And we're basically troll people."

"Who shower in a swamp," I said, bursting into obnoxious laughter. I couldn't believe the supremely sophisticated level of banter I was enjoying with this ten-year-old! He was really good at making fun of himself. Was I falling in love? With my cousin?

After our belly laughs had died down and Cara asked us three times what it was we were laughing at to no avail, Knox and I exchanged a look that I SWEAR was him telling me that he knew that I knew that he was my half brother. I hadn't found much hard evidence yet, and my probing at dinner was clearly getting me nowhere, but there was something in his eyes that said it. They said exactly what I wanted to hear.

I'm the gay little brother you've spent your entire life begging your father for. It's me. Hello.

SEVEN

Is Twitter Still a Thing?

I was really bored the next day. Like really, really, really, really bored. And really, really, REALLY annoyed. Maybe I was ovulating? I get *extra*-annoyed when I'm ovulating. That's a fun thing about me. Knox and Cara were at school, Veronica was at work, and I was certainly not about to just chill at the house with Donna. I had to get out of there to distract myself from the familial drama that was occupying my brain.

The more I thought about the whole Knox Maternity Mystery the more I wanted to scream. My mom is literally the worst. Even if it turned out that my grandfather was wrong and that my mom wasn't Knox's biological mother, I still resented her for being the type of person that she is.

Not to get tooooooooooooooooo real or whatever, but since meeting her, I've been of the mind that my mother did me a huge favor by not introducing herself to me until I was twenty-five. She would have been constantly disappointing me. But maybe that would have been better in some ways. Being around someone who was perpetually letting me down may have taught me a lesson. It would have been a lot easier to get over the fact that my mother was shitty, just by seeing her for who she truly was. I could have made my own judgment about her instead of building up this story in my little child head about what a great person she might be if she just came back into my life. As a child I was sad about all the things she missed out on. My dad and Mabinty (my childhood nanny/BFF/COO of Babe Walker Industries) were trying to protect me by pretending she didn't exist or something. I see what they were trying to accomplish, but maybe it was a bad call?

And now Knox is potentially involved in her whole mess. I didn't know if I'd ever be able to bring myself to tell him if I found out that he hadn't actually come out of Vee's . . . V. He has a great mom. She cared for him and put his needs first. Breaking that bond would be horrible. But, like . . . shouldn't he know the truth at some point? Fuck, I wish I'd never come to Maryland. No good deed . . .

I checked Instagram, tweeted something (is Twitter still a thing?), and then looked to see if there was a SoulCycle anywhere near Veronica's house. Surprise, surprise . . . there was most definitely not a SoulCycle near her house, but I did find a cute place online called the "Y." I'd never heard of it before but it sounded very chic. They had a gym, swimming pool, and yoga studio there. How bad could it be?

Smash cut to me at the Y, which it turns out was short for the YMCA, which was short for the Young Men's Christian Association, which was long for unchic. Brown carpet + fluorescent lighting + low ceilings + a sad-looking staff = me questioning what the fuck I was doing in Maryland. This was definitely not SoulCycle. Even more annoying than all the beigeness was the fact that the next yoga class wasn't scheduled until that evening. I had to settle for a water aerobics class that was about to start.

Side note: I DO NOT fuck with public pools/hot tubs. NO exceptions. No way, no how, no God, no thank you. Plus, my body situation was unclear due to the fact that I'd been eating lots of things that were not smoothies over the past few days. And I was quickly learning that Maryland was not known for its salads. Is it that hard to make organic produce available to the masses?

I paid the ten-dollar entry fee and headed into the indoor pool area. As I entered I was assaulted by the smell of chlorine and the sight of bodies.

So.

Many.

Bodies.

No judgments! But let's just say that there were a lot of different body stories happening in that pool area. A LOT. And they were all literally disgusting, but I'm not judging anyone. But seriously, they were sick. Like, insane. I scanned the huge glassed-in pool looking for the instructor of this class and something caught my eye. It was a guy. It was a guy in a bathing suit. It was a guy, in a bathing suit, who was actually . . . hot. Not like *hot* hot. But, like . . . Okay, fine, he was hot. My eye just finds beauty wherever I am. What can I say? Half blessed, half cursed.

I headed in his direction to get a closer look, while pretending that I didn't notice him. I was secretly hoping he was the instructor. He was invitingly cute in a really regular way. He was, like, six foot something tall, dark hair, and a crazy body. In the face, he looked like a cross between Scott Foley and Scott Speedman, the two love interests in the vintage TV classic *Felicity*, which coincidentally I'd been watching on Netflix. (Watch it. It's vvvv chic times ten minus three when the hair thing happens.)

I named him "Scotts" in my mind, because that made the most sense. As I approached him, he was putting goggles on and stretching his arms. Scotts was actually really fucking hot and his skin was a nice tan color, which, for this time of year in Maryland, was somehow reassuring for me. He smiled at me as I walked by. Nice teeth. Great smile. He didn't need to smile but he did because he was a decent human being, obvi. I responded with my standard half smile/half smirk/half wink/half glare/it might look like nothing but I'm definitely moving my face muscles. I know that math doesn't add up, but just go with it. Guys love it, so just let me do my thing. It's not about logic.

We definitely had a moment. A very short, but distinct moment. Then he dove straight into the pool and actually splashed me a little bit. I wasn't mad. Which was very weird because I hate being surprised by liquids. But Scotts got a pass.

"Ma'am," someone called out from across the pool.

I looked toward the source of a terrorizingly loud voice: a human being who can only be described as a Richard Simmons impersonator but obese. This person was calling out in my direction, but I was confused because I most certainly am not old enough to be perceived as a "ma'am." I'd been referred to as "miss" or "young lady," but MA'AM was a nunca. I prayed this person was not talking to me.

"Hon, are you here for my twelve thirty?" he asked, looking directly at me.

"I'm sorry? Are you talking to me?"

"Yes, girl! You. You in the head-to-toe Y-3 walking on my pool surface with sneakers."

He knows fashion. I felt immediately more comfortable with this creature.

"Is it an aerobics class?"

"Yes, hon. Water aerobics."

"Is it starting now?"

"You got it. I'm D'Angelo. Better go get into your suit, girl, or you're gonna miss it."

First of all, a white person named D'Angelo is simply remarkable.

"Oh. I'm going to be skipping the aquatic portion of today's class," I told him.

"The whole class is in the water."

"Yeah, well, that's not really gonna work for me as I don't ever get in public pools."

D'Angelo gave me a smile that said *fuck you* but also *it's okay.*

"I think I'll stand just outside of the pool and do all the movements out here."

"That's fine with me, but the point of water aerobics is for the pool water to create resistance against your muscl . . . I can tell by the look on your face that you don't care what I'm talking about so I'm gonna go 'head and start class."

"Thank you, D. I'm looking forward to this."

There were four older women in the class with me. All of them chose to be in the actual water. They were all wearing one-piece suits and little head condoms, or whatever they were. Each one of them seemed genuinely happy to be there. They were all smiling. It was kind of strange because they would smile at me when they looked at me, but they were also just smiling at each other and at D'Angelo. Like they were just happy people. Their default mode was SMILE. It made me a little angry. As the music started (Madonna, "Ray of Light," LOLZ) and I began mimicking the movements, I became starkly aware of how odd this whole situation was.

I, Babe Walker, was standing in front of a pool full of people from Maryland, basically dancing, by myself, to a Madonna song. But the weirdest part about it was that I wasn't stopping. I was somehow compelled to do this. D'Angelo was right about the resistance or whatever because it was barely a workout, but there was something meditative about it that kept me going. Ratchet tai chi. From the outside of the pool it must have looked like I was teaching the class or having a slow, balletic seizure.

But I didn't care what people were thinking. Was "not giving a fuck" about what others think of you contagious?

Almost everyone I knew in LA was constantly trying to prove how much they *didn't give a fuck* about what people thought/said about them, while simultaneously secretly giving the MOST fucks. People in LA are so full of shit, and I was part of that. I wouldn't have been caught dead doing something like this back home. I felt like I was in a dream. Nothing was bothering me about this whole scenario. Not even the fact that Scotts could probably see me doing my moves. If you're not self-conscious in the presence of a really hot guy, then there is something seriously wrong with you. Or at least I used to think so.

D'Angelo's soundtrack turned out to be MAJOR. ABBA, The Village People (ironic, but most likely completely planned by Miss D'Angelo himself), The Police, Donna Summer. I was living; the elderly women in the pool were LIVING. D was an emotional Sherpa, guiding us through our workout journey. "Now wave both arms up and down, up and down, great job, Phyllis! Glory, stick with me, honey." The class was flying by until I heard someone scream.

"HELP!!!!!!"

I looked over to the other side of the pool and saw a crowd of people starting to form around something on the ground.

"Someone call 911!!!" another voice yelled.

Honestly, I was kind of annoyed. I was really getting into

this fucking class and now some old person or child had to go and die on the side of the pool? There was no way this wasn't going to derail my enjoyment of this class, not to mention ruin my heart rate's cardio cal-burn.

"Can you turn off the music for me, hon?" D'Angelo asked.

"Sure," I replied.

I turned off his Jambox/Sonos/Beats Pill little guy that he had going and started walking slowly over to the crowd of people that was forming around the corpse. It was, like, fifteen people at this point. My curiosity pushed me right to the front of the group so I could see what was happening.

"Holy fuck. Scotts is dead!" I yelled.

There he was. Hot Scotts was just lying on his back next to the pool. He looked dead as FUCK. He skin was gray and turning transparent in some spots and the amount of breathing he was doing was none. Very, very similar to a dead person.

"Do you know him well?" a tall man, wearing a Speedo, asked me.

"I mean, kind of," I replied.

"Yeah. That guy's dead. I'm really sorry. He's not breathing at all. Jesus," he continued.

"What happened? Did anyone see what happened to him? Did he just drown?" I asked.

"No. I saw him get out of the pool. He looked out of sorts and then he just fell over onto the tile. Lifeless," a lifeguard responded. "I think he hit his head."

"I was just hanging out with him before he started doing his laps. He seemed really happy. Like, the happiest I've ever seen him. It's just so sad. Death is all around us, you know?" I felt really good about my mini-eulogy.

Someone else was now giving Scotts mouth-to-mouth. I didn't know how to feel. Was I supposed to be sad that Scotts was dead now? I barely knew him. Was I being tested? Was there a lesson to be learned here? So many questions and so little time. Scotts was not responding to the CPR at all. What I did know was that there was literally nothing I could do to help him. In fact, I felt like I was actually kind of in the way by standing there, so I decided that I could best help Scotts in his time of need by leaving . . . immediately.

When I got back in my car I YouTube'd the opening credits to *Felicity* and thought about Scotts. He was so filled with joy in the short time I knew him. But he was probably in a better place now. As the ambulance arrived at the Y, I let one semiforced tear fall from my left eye directly onto my iPhone screen. It was really a nice moment for me.

On the drive home I found myself thinking about Knox and the fragility of life. Life was painful enough. Was there really anything good that could come from me telling Knox that Donna was most likely his real mom? Would that make him a happier person? A more fulfilled human being? I couldn't do it. I couldn't hurt him like that. Then I stopped at a nail salon I'd seen on the way to the Y, and I got a very quality mani/pedi by a beautiful Korean princess named Su-bin. She told me I looked like a movie star, and then I fell asleep in the pedicure chair for three hours.

She just let me sleep. Thanks, Su-bin.

EIGHT

I Don't Want Butter Cancer.

I woke up the next day to a gorgeous presummer sunny-as-fuck morning. I was in a fabulous mood for no real reason. Love when that happens. As I came downstairs for a smoke, I noticed Donna's bags were lined up on the floor by the front door. She was standing on the back porch when I got out there. Black Saint Laurent suede jacket with fringe, white tee, black tights, black Nikes. Boring.

"Leaving so soon?" I asked her.

"I've got to get back for work."

"That's chic, because I'm sure by work you mean a shoot with fucking Bruce Weber on a farm somewhere in Montana with tons of gorgeous, rustic fauna and a painfully hot blond boy model."

Donna took a drag from her cigarette and smiled.

"How close was I?"

"Frighteningly."

"And you couldn't put your life on hold for one extra day to spend some time with your family?"

"I'm not fighting with you about this. It was really nice for us all to be together yesterday. I'm glad you were able to meet your family. Can't we just end this on a positive note?"

I took a long, weighted look at Donna, long enough to make her squirm just a little bit.

"I used to think it was cool that you were such a bitch but now I think it's sad. Not for me, I'm over that part of it. But for you."

I flicked my cigarette over the side of the deck and turned back to the door.

"I'm gonna go wake Knox and Cara up, we're going shopping today. Have a wonderful shoot."

Donna didn't respond, and we never said bye before she left.

"Knox?" I whispered into the dark room at the top of the stairs. His room was kept neat. No signs of a ten-year-old boy, no posters on the wall, no fucking lava lamp or anything basic like that. It looked more like an IKEA catalogue than a real room in the real world. Or at least what I'd imagine an IKEA catalogue to look like.

He was sleeping quietly, folded into a ball in the corner of his twin bed. Navy-and-white sheets. Down pillows. Better than the guest bed. Maybe I'd request to sleep in his bed for the rest of my stay. No. Too much.

Waking him felt like a crime. He was so precious there, probably right in the middle of a REM cycle, but he'd asked me to wake him up as soon as I got up, so wake him up I would.

"KNOX!" I screamed.

He literally jumped out of bed. He was wearing black leggings and an extralong T by Alexander Wang shirt/dress. I mean, I used to have the same shirt and I wore it as a dress. It really was a dress, not a shirt. He was wearing a dress. It was major.

"AAAAaarrrrggghhhhhh!!!" Knox screamed back at me like a wild gorilla defending her band. A group of gorillas *is* called a band. And FYI a group of cockroaches is called an intrusion and a group of dolphins is a pod. Google it.

"Ohmigod!! You scared the shit out of me."

"Sorry, babes! Just wanted to get you up so we could start going through and doing that closet edit we'd talked about. You know, before we shop. I need to know what type of canvas we're working with. Capiche?"

He looked slightly stunned. I think he was still half-sleeping.

"Okay," I said, putting my hand on his shoulder and leading him to the bathroom in the hall. "Take a shower, get your shit together, and let me know when you're ready."

"Okay."

"In ten minutes."

"OKAY."

"Don't fuck around in there. We have a lot of ground to cover, and I'm only in town for one more day."

Knox shut the door to the bathroom. With it closed, I noticed a framed needlepoint hanging from a small hook on the front of the bathroom door. It said, "Cleanliness is next to Godliness, so be Godly today!"

I took it down and threw it into a bush outside the house.

When Knox was ready I met him back in his room, and we started sorting through his wardrobe.

"So you walk all of your neighbors' dogs after school and use the money to buy clothes and cooking stuff online. That's one of the most beautiful stories I've ever heard," I said to Knox as I folded an adorable robin's-egg Lacoste polo and placed it in the Yes pile.

"The mall here isn't the cutest. You'll see later. So yeah,

I have to find everything online. And Mom lets me do it on my own now so it's pretty much awesome."

"I want to cry."

"Why? Don't cry, please."

"Ew, I'm not actually going to. I'm just super moved right now by your perseverance, dedication, and overall commitment to not be basic. Despite your surroundings, upbringing, and supposed fate. You're literally changing history by wearing those shorts to school."

I pointed to a pair of girl's floral Marc by Marc Jacobs jeans that Knox had cut into a pair of shorts. He'd also clearly washed and treated them because their wear was meticulously and beautifully weathered.

"I had Cara drive over them a bunch of times in Mom's car."

"Genius. I used to make Mabinty do that for me when I would get new white Converse Chucks. We had to wear them in PE at my elementary school and there's truly nothing more off-putting than a spotless pair of Converse Chucks. They can make you look like a sad wardrobe lady at the Disney Channel dressed you."

Knox broke out in laughter. He was eating up everything I said. This made me feel wonderful, obviously. But it also made me feel sad for him because he hadn't realized yet that I was basically a bitch who lied most of the time. But being around him did soften me a little. It's not like I had a crush on him because no, but it really was something similar. Minus the sex thoughts. He just made me feel excited to be alive. When we were hanging out, exchanging brilliances, it felt like the time actually meant something. Unlike being back in LA arguing with Genevieve about why she shouldn't eat sushi more than four times a week, or with Roman about why owning more than two Range Rovers made him look like he had a small dick. Which he doesn't AT ALL, making everything that much more frustrating. We literally had that argument and he still bought the third Range Rover, a navy one, claiming that it was for his live-in CrossFit trainer. Lies.

"I haven't ever said this to anyone because I don't actually think I've ever felt this about someone, but I am fucking impressed by your whole approach to life."

"K," he said quietly after a few dull ticks from his bedroom wall clock. "That's weird."

"Is it?"

"I think so."

"Why?"

"Because I'm so much younger than you. And you live in LA, which is, like, a real place, unlike this dump."

"Yeah, this place is a piece of shit."

"I know. And you have a life and write books and have really nice and cool stuff and good taste and you're famous."

"I'm not famous."

"Yeah you are."

"Okay, fine, a little bit. But don't tell people that. It's gauche as fuck to be famous."

"Okay."

"Thanks."

"Uh, sure. And, like, you're just—"

"I can't take any more compliments," I blurted, interrupting him. "It's making me feel weird. I haven't done anything with my life lately. My stepmother told me I need to get my act together and find a new mantra, so hearing nice things about myself is just creeping me out right now. I don't mean to take it out on you, sorry, let's just do this closet edit. Okay?"

Knox nodded his head and went back to pulling out shirts from the chest of drawers by his bed.

"Sorry, Knox. I think being around Donna has me in my feelings in all sorts of ways. I don't ever talk to her, let alone see her."

"She's pretty nice, though."

"Yeah. That's how she seems. And, like, at the end of the day, it doesn't even matter if she's nice or not because she's so hot and so thin and is still a working model, so it shouldn't matter how she treats me . . . us. But she is my mom."

"I get it."

"Yeah, you get it."

But did he really get it? If Donna was, in fact, Knox's mom, then yes he really would get it. I didn't know what to say next so I just stopped talking. I leaned over to the stereo on Knox's floor and turned the music louder. It was an old Miley Cyrus song.

"I love this song," Knox said a few moments later.

"I hate it."

The mall was about a twenty-minute drive from their house and Veronica was kind enough to let me borrow her car to get us there. I left the headlights of my rental on all night and ran the battery out, so that was no longer an option. Another reason not to rent cars. Vee's was a large hybrid minivan-SUV type thing in an odd green/gray/horrible color so I wore huge sunnies and an Hermès scarf around my head, in case anyone noticed me driving it, because *hello*. We parked far from the entrance, and I smoked half of a joint that I found in my bag on the walk over. I knew I'd need to be a little sedated to deal with the inner truths of a real, American, noncoastal-town mall. I didn't know what type of looks, smells, and sensations I'd be encountering once inside. So yeah, I medicated. Sue me. It was mostly so Knox wouldn't have to see me have a panic attack.

For the first ten mall minutes, I didn't say anything. I don't even know if I was breathing. I just took it all in 'cause

I was, like, really fucking high. The first thing I noticed was that the place smelled like chicken. The food court (is that what it's called?) must've been nearby and its essence was pumped through the entire building. It was like I was being forced to eat with my nose. I also took note of the jarring white light and the remarkable amount of girls in Uggs. Knox had convinced me to walk through hell with him. But that's what you do for family.

After I bought him several fabulous complete looks at Nordstrom (I did my best), we went to this chef-supply store and I bought him a really chic chef-knife bag made of weathered Italian leather. It stores all of his super sharp knives in a roll. Then we decided we should see a movie. Or rather, he decided he wanted to see a movie. He chose something scary about the end of the world, which I'd normally never ever ever force myself to sit through, but Dwayne "The Rock" Johnson was starring in it so I obliged. I wanna fuck him. So do you. Try to say you don't want to fuck him. Whatever.

"I'm surprised people allow themselves to eat popcorn with butter," I said to lil' Knoxie as we took our seats in the biggest theater I'd ever seen. Everything in malls is so large, it's fascinating!

"I know. It's not good for me, but I hardly ever do it."

"But, like—"

"So fuck it," he said, sure of himself. I just turned and faced forward.

"Your body, your life," I said as the lights dimmed and the trailers started.

The movie was boring—people screaming, buildings dying, helicopters, dogs, a Kylie Minogue cameo—but not as boring as it would have been if I was cold sober. Thank God for my little surprise friend that I found in my bag. I was kind of hoping that I'd fall asleep like I do normally when I see movies, but about thirty-five minutes into the film, something strange took place.

So I'd just taken a sip of my "seltzer" (they didn't carry extralarge bottles of San Pellegrino at the concessions counter), and Knox handed me his huge paper bag of popcorn as if we'd been sharing it the entire time. I took it from him, dipped my little hand into the pile of yellow, crunchy stuff, and retrieved a mouthful. Now, if I'd then thrown it at Knox's face and laughed hysterically or even secretly dumped it in the purse of the woman next to me, that would've made sense and fit naturally into the overall Babe Walker narrative, but that's not what happened.

I ate the full hand of popcorn. You heard me. I mouthed, tongued, chewed, and swallowed the mall theater popcorn that was literally still dripping with synthetic butter product. I actually did this. This is my confession to you.

Well, actually, the confession has more to do with how it tasted and what I felt while performing this truly daring and admittedly lowbrow stunt: it was delicious. It was fucking delicious as fucking fuck.

I'd never had movie popcorn, let alone popcorn with butter. I knew butter spray was a thing that existed but I'd never partaken because I don't want butter cancer. I like living too much. But today was not like every other day. My guard was down, I was under the influence of Knox and Maryland and basicness and weed, and I just let it happen.

Upon contact, my lips curled naturally around the heap of yellow kernels. They hungrily pulled the mouthful in toward the back of my throat with help of my tongue, leaving streaks of salt in their path of delicious destruction. My mouth was being terrorized by an army of taste, a murder of wrong, a tsunami of no. Yet, in that shining moment of living quite frankly on the edge of glory, I thrived.

"This is what this fucking tastes like?!" I said at full volume to Knox. Someone shooshed me. I giggled.

"I know. It's amazing, right?"

"AMAZING."

While on a pee break from the movie I checked my phone and ended up getting into an intense group convo with Roman and Genevieve. I sat on the toilet and texted for almost twenty minutes. Knox was rightfully confused when I returned. Hey, I was stoned out of my actual brain. Time didn't really exist at the time.

There were two missed texts from Roman.

Roman Babe? Gen?

Roman Hit me up when you get this. Emergency.

Babe What's happening.

Babe I'm peeing.

Babe It feels amazing.

Babe I ate butter.

Roman Are you high?

Babe No

Roman But like?

Babe Yes.

Roman Okay it's fine. I need to vent.

Babe Go off bitch

Gen Hey I'm here. What's up losers

Babe I ate butter, Roman was about to vent.

Gen Got it.

Gen Proceed.

Roman So I was at Joan's on Third for breakfast today and I ran into Mikey Dutton

Gen NO

Roman Yes bitch. I was sitting outside ya know at one of the little tables, enjoying an americano with almond milk and a small bowl of egg salad with tabasco with my new friend Lukas who works at the front desk of my chiropractor's office, we're maybe fucking but that's another story, whatever he's super hot. I'm sitting there laughing at Lukas's boring stories about his trip to Kuwait or Egypt or something and I hear someone behind me go "Roman?????"

Gen NO

Roman Yes bitch. And you know I knew immediately who the voice belonged to. I contemplated not turning around and just ignoring it but Lukas was looking at me, waiting for me to turn around and say hi back. I didn't know what to do. My adrenaline was pumping through my pores. I could either get really sweaty and gross and awk in front of Lukas who I REALLY wanted to fuck after breakfast, or I could turn around and face this feces-breathing dragon from hell himself. So I turn around and there he is and he's smiling from ear to fucking ear and he's wearing a FULL look from the

Jeremy Scott Flintstones collection which you know is my least favorite JS collection

Gen NO

Roman Yes bitch. I shit you not. This queen was just standing there looking at me, waiting for me to say something.

Gen So what'd you say? I hope you fucking slapped him across the face. What he's done to you! AND what he said to you at that Grammys after party last year was one of the darkest, cruelest, shadiest things I've ever heard. You don't deserve to EVER run into him. You just don't deserve it. You're a good person Roman.

Roman I know I am.

Gen Really. You have such a huge heart.

Roman Thanks, Gen. You're being nice, it's weird.

Gen I hope you stabbed him.

Roman LOL

Roman I fucking wanted to. Trust.

Gen What happened? Were tables thrown?

Babe Wait.

Babe I may or may not have just fallen asleep while peeing.

Gen Ew

Roman Ew Babe. Where are you?

Babe Promise you'll still talk to me if I tell you

Roman I promise

Gen I don't

Babe I'm in a public bathroom stall at a movie theater in a mall in Maryland

Roman WHAT WHY

Gen NO

Babe I tried to tell you guys before but no one wanted to listen

Roman Fine. Brief pause to my story so you can tell us why in the actual fuck you are where you are

Babe I came here to meet Donna's side of the family.

Babe Donna's side of MY family I guess I should say

Gen Intense

Roman But cute

Roman I think it's good you're doing that

Babe I guess

Babe But there's a lot of butter here

Gen I'm sure there's butter everywhere. Scary food is king in the non-coastal states.

Roman Genevieve, Maryland is on the east coast

Gen It is?

Roman 100%

Gen Whatever

Roman Babe I want details later but I need to finish my story

Babe K

Babe But wait who's Mikey Dutton?

Roman LOL

Roman You've met him before. He's a "stylist" and also my arch nemesis from CrossFit that PISSED IN THE GAS TANK OF MY CAR when he found out I'd been chosen to be a judge on RuPaul's Drag Race this season and he hadn't

Roman He claims it was his biggest goal in life and I stole it from him

Gen Love that fucking show

Babe Same. So I get it. But ew.

Babe I think this sounds familiar.

Babe Where did I meet him?

Roman At Pepo

Babe What's pepo

Roman That spanish restaurant with the hot bus boys

Babe Pepo. Of course. They are hot

Roman SO hot

Roman I hadn't seen Mikey since the day he called me basic at that Grammys party in front of legit 3 million people

Gen I still can't believe he said that

Babe That's all he said?

Roman What do you mean that's all

Roman Imo that's the single most offensive thing you could say to a person

Babe Really?

Babe It doesn't seem like the MOST to me

Babe But hey I'm very stoned right now

Babe I should go back to the theater. My little cousin is in there

Roman Let me finish. It gets good.

Roman So I look at him, I stand up, overcome by a strange sense of cunty yet calm confidence, I walk over to him and I whisper this: That hello was the last word you'll ever say to me. You are a major source of negativity in my life, you ruin my day, you're a child, you're an actual diaper filled with doo doo, you're the worst, leave me alone

Gen NO

Babe Omg

Babe So unlike you to get worked up, romie

Roman I know it was nuts but I knew that if I didn't handle it swiftly and calmly, he'd make a scene

Babe Love swiftness

Roman And just before I could turn around and walk back to my table, he throws his entire, large iced-latte in my face

Babe SHUT

Gen UP

Roman So I punched him square in the jaw

Babe I'm gonna scream

Babe I am screaming

Babe In this bathroom

Babe ROMAN WHAT at Joan's????!!!!!

Gen I'm proud of you Romie

Roman Thanks.

Roman I'm anti-violence or whatever but I'm also anti fuckboy

Roman Anyway I gotta go and Babe you need to get out of that bathroom

Babe So true

Gen Yeah wtf

Gen Love you guys x

NINE

Still Thinking About the Popcorn I Ate in Chapter Eight.

I felt really guilty about eating the popcorn. Like, it was all I thought about for the entire drive home from the mall, the entire rest of the evening, and probably the entire rest of my life. Eating popcorn with butter is honestly just like doing cocaine. *(New mantra?)* You have some, it's amazing, you feel amazing, and then all you can think about is having more. Like, right then. It becomes a need. Elemental to your very being. You *have* to have more popcorn/cocaine because it's the best thing you've ever put into your body and why wouldn't you want to have more of it? I'd always wondered why people *actually* get fat, and now, for the first time, I had a glimpse of how that could happen. But, I had two cigarettes, two generous imaginary lines of coke, and a HUGE bottle of Fiji for dinner and it made me feel much better. I was back.

The more time that I spent with Knox, the more connected I felt to him. He was Mini-Me and he got 75 percent of my pop-culture references, which is an extremely high percentage for this particular geographical region or really anywhere, especially considering he was seventeen years younger than me. Knox understood who I was. He didn't judge me for being specific in my needs as a human being. He never scoffed at my dietary restrictions. He looked up to me. It was a strange experience, a wild sensation. In LA, no one would dare act like they looked up to me. But Knox was just proud to be my cousin. He genuinely appreciated me for . . . me.

It made me feel good in a way I wasn't accustomed to feeling. But the feelings were also complicated by the fact that I knew in my heart that I was keeping a huge secret from Knox. He looked to me for total realness. I wondered sometimes if I was the first person in his life who was willing to level with him. But maybe I wasn't being as real with him as he thought. I needed to sort this out. I needed to get confirmation that Donna wasn't Knox's mom. I spent the rest of the night Googling DNA testing methods and came up with some viable options for determining which vagina Knox had emerged from.

The next morning I was up bright and early at 11:15 a.m. I drove to Starbucks in the car I found in the driveway, got coffee, and then drove to a little river near Veronica's house. It was quiet, smelled like outsideness, and I was feeling fucking *namaste* as fuck. I started to ponder an idea I'd been playing with for a book or a TV show about a lipstick lesbian who is running for president. I do that sometimes. I just jot down ideas I have in my phone and then I get really fucking excited about them and obsess over them and think about them constantly. Then I never do anything about turning them into a reality because without fail, every single time I look back at these ideas after a month or so, they're complete shit and I'm shocked that I ever even considered them as legitimate. I get high a lot.

As I was drawing a sketch of The Lesbian President's inauguration look (spoiler alert: she wins the election in the pilot!), I got a text from a rando number:

410-443-XXXX Hi Babe. It's V

Babe Hi!!!!!!!!!!!!!!!!!!!!!

410-443-XXXX Need a big favor from you

Babe Sorry I can't

Babe JK.

Babe Just kidding.

Babe Whats up?

410-443-XXXX When is your flight back to LA?

Babe Late tonight

410-443-XXXX Shit. Ok.

Babe Why?

410-443-XXXX It's fine don't worry about it.

Babe V. Whats up?

410-443-XXXX I have to go to Cara's school tonight for conferences and I just got asked to cover someone's shift.

Babe You want me to go to Cara's school?

410-443-XXXX Honestly its fine I know you have to leave town. youve been really helpful already with the kids

Babe I can do it. I'll change my flight.

410-443-XXXX Really?

Babe Yeah. NO problem!

Babe Who is this btw

410-443-XXXX V

410-443-XXXX Veronica

Babe OK thought so. Cool! All good love you

Question: What exactly did I mean when I said "no problem"? It was actually a huge problem because I hate schools and I hate people. This was a combo of both. But I felt for Vee. She was a single mom, she seemed to have done a pretty good job raising these kids, and I wasn't really in a huge rush to get back to LA. In fact, it had been kind of nice to be out of town for the past few days. Then I had an idea.

Our gay heroine is not only chic and only wears neutrals, but she is a single mom. Like Veronica. And her niece is an international bestselling author. An author of children's books, because fiction!

Once I had my idea jotted down, I checked Instagram, smoked a cigarette, logged onto Grindr using Roman's password because it's fun to talk to real-life gays and see what types of dick pics they'll send you, and tried skipping a stone in the river. That last part about the stone is actually not true.

I knew I'd have to rush if I was going to make it home to get ready and then to the school on time for tonight's big event. I scooped my life up and pumped my way out of that little river park, snagging my favorite Rick Owens crepe drop-rise jumpsuit on a bush on my way down the path to the car. The rip was too big and could never be fixed so I just slipped out of it, left it to the wilderness gods, and drove home in my underwear. I knew there was no room for that type of mess in my life at that juncture. So, bye.

I was pulling into Veronica's driveway when my phone ding'd.

Genevieve Did you hear that Remy died?

Babe Our shoe lady at Barneys?

Genevieve Yes!

Babe Stop

Genevieve I'm serious. She drove her little convertible off the PCH

Babe Stop

Genevieve Before that, she lit her boyfriend's apartment on fire. Like full arson moment

Babe Stop

Genevieve And supposedly stole a bunch of Celine mules and gave them to homeless women downtown

Babe Stop

Genevieve I think she was a little crazy

Babe I would've had NO idea. We loved Remy!

Genevieve Loved

Genevieve When are you coming back? I'm over everyone here. Roman is out of his mind. I can't. Do you miss me?

Babe Never coming back and don't really miss you

Genevieve K

Babe Love you call me tomorrow

Genevieve Love you

I chose to wear all black to the Back to School gala in honor of my late shoe saleslady, Remy Something. She was a good woman who never lost composure when I screamed at her or cried while in her presence, which was often. I'll miss you, Rem.

I threw my hair up in a high, tight pony, tossed myself into an epic pair of Miu Miu pumps that I'd forgotten I even brought, and took a shot from a bottle of vodka I found in Veronica's freezer. I was excited to finally see what *going out* looked like in the wilds of Maryland.

"There are a lot of men in khakis here. Is that normal?" I asked the young mom standing next to me by the refreshments table. She smiled and nodded. It looked like she wanted to say something, but she ultimately chose to simply ice me and walked away.

Whatever. Being a fake mom for the night was already a

snooze. And this was not an event. We were in a gym. I sat down at a table, pulled lipstick out of my clutch, and did that for a while. When I looked up I saw a familiar face. I thought it was the hot dead guy from the pool, Scotts, but he died, so it couldn't have been him. I walked up to him anyway. He smelled good in a super basic way. No cologne, just Dove or Dial soap. It was definitely a weird smell for a dead person to have.

"Hey, I'm Babe. Didn't I see you die the other day?"

"Pardon?"

I repeated the exact same sentence verbatim but slower.

"Ohhhhh. At the pool?"

"Yes, at the pool. The site of the accident."

"Did we meet? You look super familiar."

"There were glances and unnecessary but welcomed smiles."

"Right. That was you. Well, I'm fine, yeah. It was scary, though."

"And now you're what, like, the walking dead? It's not clear."

"No, I'm okay. It's happened before. It's a nerve thing. I don't know, I'm bad at going to the doctor. D'Angelo gave me mouth-to-mouth. It was wonderful to wake up to that face. Those kinky curls. You know."

I looked at him for a while, contemplating what to say

next. I'd never spoken to a real live dead person before. Ghosts, yes. I was even molested by two ghosts in New Orleans once—long story. But never the living dead.

"You're hot even though you're dead."

"Still trying to make this dead joke work. Okay. Bold move, I can respect that."

"I don't know what you're talking about," I said.

He gave me a look that let me know he had no idea what *I* was talking about.

"You know what?" I said, tossing my hair over my shoulder. "Let's start over."

"I like that plan."

"So."

"So . . . you're Babe? This is your actual name?"

"Yes. And you're really not dead? You swear on your own life?"

"Swear on my family's life, and I happen to genuinely like my family."

"Okay. I mean, this is gonna take some getting used to because to be quite fucking honest, I initially walked over here because I was so fascinated by the hot zombie boyfriend in our presence and I wanted to see what the vibes were. But now you're saying that you were resuscitated. So you're just, like, alive, I guess? Like me?"

"Yep."

"That's boring."

"Sometimes it is. Yes, sometimes being alive is very boring. That is correct."

"Most of the time it is. Like right now I'm a little bit bored. I was expecting much more from a Back to School Night. Growing up, my dad would always come home wasted from my schools' Back to School Nights."

Scotts looked a little confused. "Well, tonight is actually parent-teacher conference night."

"What?" I asked, shocked, disappointed, and more bored than before.

"Who are your kids? Maybe they're in my class."

"Oh, no. No no no no no. I don't have kids. Cara and Knox are my cousins, and I'm just here filling in for their mom, Veronica. She had to work late. I'm from LA. I'm a writer. This is not my life. I'm here as a joke, basically. But I did think this would actually be cute and fun but I was clearly wrong. Okay. I'm gonna stop talking now 'cause you don't care and I definitely don't care. Okay, so you can say something now."

Scotts chuckled. "Ah, I see. I have Cara in my English class. She's a super bright kid. A little dark. She's bright and dark. As a lot of teenagers are."

"Um. Okay. Cool?"

"I'm an English teacher here. Pretty thrilling stuff."

"So you're saying I'm not here to drink and talk shit about kids and then leave?"

"Well, typically on conference night we go over each kid's progress in their respective courses with their parents. But I wouldn't hate if we went for a drink after. Thoughts?"

"I like your style," I said with a real smile. He liked me.

"Is that a yes?"

"It's a 'not no.' "

"I can work with that. I'm Scott by the way."

"Stop."

He looked around the room, extremely confused now.

"Stop what?"

"Before we met tonight I called you that in my head because you look like a cross between Scott—"

"Speedman and Foley."

"Yes!"

"I've gotten it before. And thank you," he said, smiling, "I take that as a huge compliment. They're babes."

"They *are* babes. So am I. I'm a Babe."

We both laughed.

"Good one. Funny," Scott said.

"Thanks. I'm one of the quickest people I know. Just a heads up."

"I'll consider myself warned. So." He glanced at his watch, not a vintage Rolex, but okay. "I have to go to my next appointment. And I believe I'm actually supposed to have my conference about Cara in fifteen minutes with, well, I guess with you? So, see you then?"

"Oh. Sure. Yeah, see you then."

"Okay!" Scott said and started to walk away.

"Hey, Scott? How do I know which teacher to go see now?"

He pointed to a board on the wall with a big grid on it.

"Have a look at the schedule over there. See you soon, Babe."

"Ciao."

After dying a little for saying ciao (I don't know, it just came out), I found my schedule of appointments on the board and made my way over to room 2054, Earth Sciences. I was going to meet Cara's biology teacher.

Mr. Young was an extremely tall and pale thing. His look/body/aura was serving me raw wax bean. Even his outfit was beige and his shoes were white and surely orthopedic. Halfway to his desk I stopped.

"You know," I said to the man, "I think I'm gonna pass. I'm not even Cara's real mom."

Mr. Young looked baffled even when I assured him that this was fine with Cara's mom and that "I simply just needed to do me."

Before exiting the brick dungeon that was that school

(honestly, no wonder this country is so fucked up if that's where children are expected to learn to be cute), I found Scott's room and slipped a note under his door.

Scott,

I left because I hate it here. I'm sorry this is your place of work. I'm sure you're a wonderful teacher. Let's make out before I leave town? 323-XXX-XXXX. Text me, zombie.

xo,

Babe

TEN
You're Hot, but Fuck You.

"Scott," I said as he sat down at the table across from me. "Scott, Scott, Scott. You're super lucky I didn't say fuck it and leave."

"Why's that?" he said with a smile. Gorgeous. I was even a little nervous for him to get there, which was weird but cute, I guess. I'd ordered a glass of rosé, which I'd almost finished already, which is not that cute, I guess.

"You're twenty minutes late."

"I'm five minutes late."

"That's not true," I informed him, holding up my phone to him so he could see the time for himself.

Scott's eyes widened, and he started laughing as soon as he looked.

"What?"

I turned the phone to me and to my horror, there was an enormous pink dick staring back at me.

"Fuck!" I shouted. Oh my God. It was a dick pic from Genevieve that she must've sent at the exact moment I was turning my phone to Scott. "Fuck. Fuck. Ew, God. I'm sorry."

"It's fine," he said through laughs, which were becoming more of a nervous, confused giggle. Straight guys don't know what to do around dicks. I can appreciate a beautiful vagina. It's weird that they can't just appreciate their natural beauty, but hey, to each his boring and straight own.

"It's nice," he managed to say. "Very pink."

I looked again.

"Very pink. So true."

Maybe Scott was a cool straight guy who actually appreciated dick. Like, as art.

"Well, sorry I'm late. We had a town meeting at school this afternoon that went on about three hours too long."

"You have town meetings here? So cute. So *Gilmore Girls*."

"No, no. That's just what the principal at our school calls them. They're long, drawn-out faculty meetings with an open-floor policy. This basically just means that Kath from the art department can talk about the healing faculties of pottery for as long as she wants. And Jackson, the music teacher who's never not high, never ceases to amaze us with his annual suggestions for ways to make the school more 'tie-dye.'"

"Jackson sounds funny. I used to know a Jackson. He was a thorn in my fucking side, and his breath smelled like something made with almond milk that might be served in a mason jar."

"Yuck."

"Extreme levels of yuck. But he meant well. And Kath just sounds like a bitch."

"She's miserable. I really wish someone would do something about her already. I think about how to do it all the time."

"Kill her?"

"Kill her, yeah. She has no family. It wouldn't even matter."

Hot. I took a long sip of my sparkling water while holding eye contact with Scott.

"Are you a murderer?" I asked, serving him my best *Law & Order: SVU*, which I believe is a show where cops ask people questions like that.

"No. I was kidding."

"Ah . . ."

"Sorry, bad joke. Kath is lovely. Odd thing going on with one of her toes on the left foot. It's literally the color of a green apple. Couldn't tell you why. But otherwise she's lovely."

"You're funny," I said. I didn't mean to. I never compliment guys that I like. It's not cute. Dammit. *Just run with it*, I told myself. *He doesn't have to know you're horrible. What if he thought you were nice? That might work.*

"I was excited to hang," Scott said.

"You know, I was, too. I didn't expect to go on any dates while I was here, but I'm learning quickly that this trip is just a series of weird but welcome surprises."

"Tell me more."

"Okay."

I ran my hand through my hair, mussing it, letting Scott know that I was totally a normal person that he should be attracted to. To be honest, I knew nothing could work between us because I would never move here, but I did need to have sex and he was a cross of Speedman and Foley.

"So I didn't meet my mom until I was about twenty-four, which is a long story that maybe I'll bless you with when I'm drunk later. So yeah, I basically don't know the crazy bitch. And she *is* crazy. She may seem put together because she's a supermodel who's still working in her late forties, but trust me, she's a mess. But she invited me here to come to her dad—my grandpa's—eightieth birthday. I accepted the invitation after much delibs because honestly, I needed to get out of Los Angeles and work on finding a mantra."

"What's a mantra?"

"Google it. So while I'm here I'm staying with Veronica—my aunt and Knox and Cara's mom—all of whom I'd never even really heard of until a week or so ago. It's just a lot of newness, a lot of wondering how I'm related to these people, and a lot of deep, deep, deep introspection."

Scott shot me the warmest of smizes and was about to tell me how he's been thinking of nothing but our upcoming date for the last day and also that my hair looked effortlessly sexy and I smelled amazing when—

"Hey, guys. What can I get you to drink, sir?"

The waitress who'd gotten me my wine was standing over the table and grinning at Scott. She put a glass of water in front of him.

"Hey. Thanks. Yeah, I'll have a beer. Whaddya got?"

"We've got Sam Adams, Bud, Bud Light, Heineken, and Yuengling on tap and Natty Boh and Modelo cans."

I touched Scott's hand.

"I don't really love when people drink beer around me. It's so burpy," I said quietly but with a sternness to let my date know that I wasn't requesting, I was insisting.

"Oh man, really? That sucks for you," Scott said with a squint of the brows to feign sympathy. He looked back up at the waitress whose name was 100 percent Quinn. Blond. Teeth. Scrunchie. Etc.

"I'll take a Yuengling, thanks so much."

"You got it, darlin'," Quinn said and left.

"You think *I'm* funny?" Scott asked.

I knew what he meant.

"You're the funny one. Jesus!" he said.

"I'm nothing if not honest. And I honestly needed you to know that if a beer was ordered, then my comfort level would plummet. But you seem to be fine with that."

"I think you're stronger than you realize. I think you can manage."

"I hope so."

Quinn was back with Scott's spiteful beverage. That was fast. Did everyone hate me today?

"So," Scott said after licking a thin coat of beer foam from his upper lip, "speaking of you being funny."

"Look," I stopped him, "I'm feeling very attacked by both you and Quinn at this point and I just don't think I can take much more bullying."

He looked like he felt bad. But then he said, "Who's Quinn?"

"Our waitress."

"Her name is Beth."

"How the fuck do you know that? Did you guys used to fuck? God, this town is unbearably small. I don't know how you cope."

"She's wearing a name tag."

"Oh."

"It says: BETH."

"Oh. Okay. Fine. That's probably her name, then, you're right."

I wrapped both of my hands around the glass of rosé in front of me and lifted it to my face like I was sipping a hot mug of tea and trying hopelessly to catch some warmth in the cold wilderness of this now very awk lunch. He was so cute and probably had the most handsome of dicks that he took great care of and I was fucking it all up. Fucking it all right up. So typical of me. I thought I'd learned this lesson. Why must I ALWAYS self-sabotage? As soon as I'm attracted to someone I immediately—

"Babe."

Scott's voice was a distant echo in my head. But it was booming.

"Babe."

It grew closer. He was pulling me out of my shame spiral.

"Babe. Are you all right? What the fuck?"

I broke out of my paralysis.

"I'm . . . I'm sorry, I just spaced out hard core."

"I saw. Are you okay?"

"Yeah, I think I'm fine."

"Okay, cool. I thought you were going Babette on me," Scott said, relieved, taking another sip of his beer.

"Excuse me?"

"Oh yeah, I read your books. Should I not have done that? You look upset."

"I'm not upset," I told him. I wasn't, really. But I felt weird. Exposed. Vulnerable. Naked.

"So you know all about Babette."

"Yeah."

"And Robert."

"Mmmmm-hmm."

Side note: Babette is the version of me that I become when I have feelings for someone. Transformation into her form is typically sudden, fast, and unavoidable. She is also a reptilian succubus from the part of hell where they keep actual monsters and gargoyles.

I took a deep breath. *Why did I write those fucking books? Why am I a writer? Can I keep nothing as sacred? Whatever. Fuck you, Scott. You're hot, but fuck you.*

"No. It's totally cool," I said, trying to convince myself that I actually felt that way. "Now I don't have to tell you about myself 'cause you basically know everything already."

"I don't think I know everything there is to know. I mean, I'd like to think that there's more to you than a series of botched vacations in exotic locales, stints in rehab, random sex around the world, and a stereotypically racist depiction of your Jamaican nanny."

It felt like Scott had literally just slapped me across the face. I slowly backed my chair away from the table and stood up. I smiled at him.

"I'm gonna run to the bathroom really quickly. BRB."

"Uh, okay."

I was embarrassed. He knew he'd crossed the line. I turned and walked toward what I thought was the bathroom door. Turned out the door was to a dark broom closet. Flustered, I asked a busboy if he could direct me to the bathroom, which he kindly did. I literally ran there and slammed the door behind me. After squeezing my eyes tightly shut for ten meditative breaths and chanting the words "Anna Dello Russo" with each exhale (she's the editor-at-large at *Vogue Nippon* and if you didn't already know that, then honestly put this down and read something else), I found the light switch with my hand and flipped it on.

There I was in the mirror. My white Saint Laurent jeans and Baja East light cashmere poncho looked flawless, but in my face I looked like a scared child version of myself. *Get it together, flawless child Babe. You're fine. You're a master of words. You are not Babette-ing. Go out there and fucking set this asshole straight. He doesn't know you. He doesn't know SHIT about your life.*

The next thing I knew, I was standing in front of Scott, my mouth was moving, words were coming out, and basics at neighboring tables were side-eyeing me, probably wondering why the model was screaming and making a scene.

". . . but the thing that really boils my blood, Scott, is your complete disregard for the fact that Mabinty Latreece Monette Mylandra Jones is a REAL human being whom I've spent the majority of my life looking up to. The fact that you think I'm 'funny' is frankly offensive if you don't have the brain capacity to appreciate the true nature of my relationship with my actual ONLY mother figure on this entire planet. Where do you get off? Racist?!"

"Babe—"

"You think you know about the world because you're a 'teacher' at a shit school in the middle of literally nowhere hell shithole America—"

"Hey, lady. Watch it now!" a man yelled from behind me.

"NO!" I yelled back at him. "This is *my* moment!"

I grabbed Scott's beer and poured the rest of it down my throat, swallowing with a gulp.

"Beast mode!" Quinn shouted from the across the room.

"No, I'm not done!" I announced. "You should know better. YOU SHOULD KNOW BETTER." I couldn't believe how loud I was getting. This was definitely not Babette, but it may have been a new version of her, a newly discovered species of *cunt from Hades*. I had no control. I'd lost it.

"Babe," Scott pleaded. "Please. I'm sorry, really. Let's go outside and talk."

"Are you crazy? Go outside with you? Why would I want to go anywhere with you? You have zero respect for me. You clearly don't appreciate the things I've been through in my life. My journey means nothing to you. I know that now. No. You don't care that my mom abandoned me before she even gave me a name. Or that I was basically forced to rape my gay male best friend in order to have sex for the first time because the rest of the guys at my school were all such enormous fuckboys. Or that my best friend Genevieve is a genuinely evil person. Or that I had a crippling shopping addiction that sent me to an EXTREMELY unchic rehab center with no robes and no koi ponds. Or that I was stalked literally across the entire European continent for months. MONTHS! Or that I'm just meeting the majority of my living family for the first time in my entire life because they were basically kept secret from me and I had to come *here* of all places to do so. Imagine what this place looks, feels, and smells like to someone who doesn't leave the coasts while in this country?! Can you imagine what this place is like for me? No! You can't. Because you live in your little bubble of a life where nothing scary happens and no one rips you apart on social media or gives your book horrible reviews or calls you racist. You have NO IDEA who Babe Walker is."

I grabbed my chair and pulled it to me, stepping one foot at a time up onto the seat. I'm not even joking, this really happened.

"Babe Walker is a queen," I said. "Babe Walker is a warrior queen!"

ELEVEN

Bless Up.

Babe Pack your shit

That was the text I sent Knox right before my cab, which smelled like soup, peeled out of the restaurant parking lot where I'd met Scott.

Knox OK

Knox Why?

Babe The MasterChef LA auditions are in two day, yes?

Knox OMG

Babe I'll be at your house in ten minutes. We're going to Los Angeles.

Knox Already packing.

Babe Don't tell your mom

Knox Never

A few minutes later, I was back at Veronica's house manically throwing clothes into my bags. We were getting le fuck outta Dodge. I realized when I was with Scott that I'd lost track of myself. I was being Boring Bitch Babe, not Fun Bitch Babe. I had to do something irrational and expensive to bring myself back to reality. So I booked two seats on the next LA flight for Knoxie and myself while I was on my way to pick him up and grab my shit.

We were at the airport an hour later. To get through security and everything, I'd forged Veronica's signature on a note that stated that I, Babe Walker, was his temporary legal guardian and his mother had given me permission to fly with him. I was basically an FBI agent.

I was drinking a gin and tonic, he'd ordered a beer (which I did not let him have because I was being responsible) and then a ginger ale. The place was pretty empty—it was a Tuesday evening, after all. Travel tip: travel on Tuesdays if you can. Less noise and fewer sad families.

"Your travel look is wonderful, by the way," I told Knox as we sipped our drinks in the lounge preflight.

"Really? Thanks. I'm not loving it."

"What's not to love?"

"I don't know, I feel like these Missoni Chucks are played. And I wanted to wear this Haider Ackermann hoodie knockoff that I found on eBay but I couldn't find it anywhere. I think my mom might've thrown it out. She says it looks like something they'd wear in *Star Wars* on the desert planet. Whatever, I had to settle for this tracksuit, which I guess is serviceable . . ."

"First of all, those sneakers are classics, they will never be played," I assured my young protégé. "And in regards to Veronica's opinion of said sweatshirt, I truly hope she wouldn't do something like that. Throwing away someone else's clothing is a hate crime, if you ask me."

"I agree. Like, let me live."

"Yeah. Let me live, Mom!"

"Mom!! Ughhh!"

Knox and I were literally best friends at this point. I wanted to cry. So emotional. So real.

"Well, cheers," I said, holding up my tumbler for him to clink it with his soda.

"Cheers, Aunt Babe."

"Whoa, whoa, whoa. Don't ever call me that again. Please. I'm not even your aunt."

"I know, I was kidding. Felt like a good time for a 'you're old' joke."

"It's never a good time for that. I'll lose it. I'm way too close to thirty to laugh at anything involving age. You'll see. It's a complete horror."

"Why? You'll make a cool old lady."

"Literally stop talking."

"Yes, ma'am."

"Ma'am?!"

"Okay, okay! I'm done."

I flipped open the copies of *Vogue* and *Harper's* I'd grabbed from the magazine rack. I like to read two magazines simultaneously when I have the space. One on each knee. And waiting in airport lounges for a flight is the perfect time and place for me to do that.

"How do you process two articles at once?" Knox asked, leaning in to have a look at what I was reading.

"I do editorials first, like this. I mentally dog-ear the articles that I want to read in the future and normally have one of my interns recite them to me while I stretch or sometimes when I'm sleeping. I still totally get it all."

"Got it."

"What time is it?" I asked, looking at my phone.

We had to go.

The plane was new, thank God. I'm so sick of old, scary, beige planes.

"This plane is cool as shit!" Knox announced to a full

first class cabin of old people who turned their old heads to look at him. So many neck wrinkles displayed at the same time in such a small place. They must be from here and not from LA, I figured, because you just don't really see that amount of neck skin in LA. We do something about it there.

"Is this your first time in first class?" I asked with literal glee. Charity work gets me so high.

"Babe, this is my first time on a plane."

"WHAT?" I shouted, wringing out the cabin's necks once again. "What a blessed day this is for you, if I may say so for myself, Sir Knoxwell."

"It's an amazing day. I almost don't care about how insanely and irreparably angry my mom's gonna be about doing this without telling her. It's worth it."

"Oh, she'll be fine. I texted her a few hours ago and cleared everything. We're good."

"Really? Okay. Good news."

"How have you never been on a plane before?"

"When I go to see my dad, we always drive. My mom doesn't really like to fly. It freaks her out, I guess."

"I've never understood people that are scared of flying. Like, of course it's scary but so is doing molly or trying uni for the first time. Who knows what's gonna happen? But that's what life is about: not knowing what's gonna happen. Am I wrong?"

The way I slurred my "I" into the end of "am" let me know I was drunk from the gin and tonic.

"I think you're drunk, Babe."

"I think you're drunk, Knox."

"I'm not."

"Yeah, whatever. I know you are. You're not the same when you drink," I said sarcastically. I was super funny when I was with Knox. It was almost like I was watching a movie and it's me but I'm playing this other woman, a woman with kids and a life.

"I'm already dying over you getting picked to be on the show and then literally slaying each and every last one of those little bitches week after week," I said to him.

"It's not gonna happen."

I could hear true doubt in his voice.

"Of course it is. I'm extremely good at picking the winner on the first episode of reality TV competition shows. And trust me, you are the winner."

"I just have no clue who the other kids will be. They might all be super good."

"They might be. And that would be annoying. But *you* are super good. Hello?"

"Whatever happens happens," he said, a bit of confidence leaking through.

"When they meet you and see your commitment to not

only your passion for food but also for just good taste in general, these dumb-as-fuck producers are going to shit themselves over you. I know how this business works and I know that the people who go far all have one thing in common: they're a brand. And you are, like, the best brand ever."

Knox didn't say anything. He nodded and took out his iPod. I watched him scroll through artists and finally click on Demi Lovato. Then I made a quick mental jot to start steering him in a different musical direction.

I think I might've overwhelmed him or gone over his head with the branding stuff. I forgot that he was just a ten-year-old boy. Ten is pretty young, I guess. I'd been collecting vintage Helmut Lang for two years by the time I was ten and I remember a friend of my dad's having a look at my archive one day and telling me that he couldn't believe I was only ten and so enterprising. He also told me that old souls ran in my family, and I never really knew what he meant. Until pretty recently, I'd fancied myself a young soul but maybe I was wrong. Like, a few days before I flew to Maryland I used my cigarette holder and told someone that they looked swell. And it made sense that Knox would also be so unique compared to his surroundings. Like me. Us old souls have a way of seeing things clearly but differently. But Knox really was still a baby. I had to remind myself sometimes.

I decided I wasn't going to tell him that I was lying about texting his mom. I hadn't texted Veronica. She would've probably gotten me arrested before we even took off for LA. I legit kidnapped Knox. I had to. I was now his Sherpa, and *MasterChef Junior* was our Everest.

When he woke up from his nap, we were almost there.

TWELVE

A Mountain of Basicness to Climb.

I was sitting outside with Roman on his second-floor terrace. He was getting a massage from his forever-masseur, Ray. Ray is a small, pear-shaped man who has worn a lace-front weave of lustrous, brown, real Indian hair since I've known him. It's a heinous sight, but the thing about massage therapists is that you don't really have to look at them, so they're free to look however they choose, so everyone's happy.

I told Roman that getting a massage while we hung out was rude, but he said he had no other time available, which I understood. It was a picture-perfect LA morning. The sun was burning as bright as God, and there was already a warm, smooth, creamy texture to the air. Normally that perfect blend of sultry temps and smog doesn't mix well until middle of summer, but it was happening already in late spring and I was not mad. Global warming is chic in its own pesky little way. If you let it be. Not mad at all. Knox was getting LA's finest treatment, just as he deserved. The little prince was inside fixing up some breakfast for all of us. We'd slept at Roman's last night after we got in. Romie was even nice enough to pick us up from the airport, which was completely unnecessary and weird of him. Did he genuinely miss me? I'd missed my number one Queen of Studs bestie. He grounded me.

"You haven't gained any weight," Roman acknowledged graciously, looking out at the Hollywood Hills. His new house was up on Appian Way in the hilly, cuter, smaller-houses, West Hollywood part of the hills.

"Did you expect me to have gained weight after spending less than one week outside of LA?"

"Um. Yeah."

"Okay, fair. Anyone else might be susceptible to that risk. I mean, Romie, there are virtually no smoothie places there."

"None? At all?"

"None that don't use dairy," I assured him.

"Jesus."

"I know. Which is really why it's so insane that he's

turned out like this," I said, pointing inside toward the kitchen, where Knox was working.

"Babe, he's a cute little gay kid from a small town. He came into this world looking for a chic way out. It's in his blood."

"First of all, that's just not true. Not every gay person is born chic. You of all people should know not to generalize your people that way. You're not even chic sometimes."

"Ugh, fine. But you know what I mean—"

"And secondly, shhhhhh, please, Romie. We haven't talked about that yet."

I hoped Knox hadn't heard Roman's comment from the kitchen. TBH, I thought Knox was gay, too. But he'd have to talk to me about it in his time for it to be a productive experience. I've seen too many people forced out of the closet at the wrong time to make that mistake with Knox. He was only ten, remember?

"But you agree, right?"

I didn't say anything.

"The boy is totally gay, Babe."

My phone ding'd. A text from Veronica.

Veronica Babe. I know you're with him. I'm freaking out. Please let me know what's happening? Are you guys okay? Just bring him back.

Veronica CALL ME

"Fine," I whispered harshly, flustered, putting my phone facedown and leaning in toward Roman's head in the massage table's cradle. "Yes. Of course I agree. He has no interest in girls whatsoever and his idol is fucking ME. But I'm not gonna act like his gayness is something he needs to confess to me. Hello? That's fucking bullshit. He's a free bitch and he'll figure it out in time. Little Knoxers has enough on his plate right now between meeting his idol/cousin/possible sister and the *MasterChef* audition tomorrow morning and being here for the first time, not to mention the fact that his sad, underprivileged, Maryland upbringing must be a constant weight on his shoulders. A burden to bear. A mountain of basicness to climb. And he's doing a really good job, okay? So why does gay or not gay even matter?"

"I mean, I was just saying. You can relax. You're not like his mom or something."

I backed away and pulled an American Spirit from Roman's pack that was sitting on the tiled table next to me. Lit it. "It's the weirdest thing," I said. "I feel something for this little queen that I've never felt for anyone. Like if he gets hurt or if someone fucks with him, then I'll have failed."

"So you, like, care about him."

"Yeah."

"And want him to be safe?"

"Right."

"And if one of you had to get hurt, you'd choose yourself over him, right?"

"That's dark. But yeah."

"Babe," Roman said with a pause that inspired weight.

"What?"

"You really think he could be your brother?"

"It's possible—"

"What are you guys talking about?" Knox said. He was standing in the door holding a platter of food.

I just smiled. No idea what to say. This was not how I wanted Knox to hear about my sneaking, suspicious, and probably completely inaccurate theory. Luckily, Roman saved me.

"Babe was being sweet and helping me with some lines I need to memorize."

"Oh, amazing. For a movie you're in?" Knox asked.

"A TV show I would *like* to be in."

Knox came out on the terrace and put the platter down before us.

"Very cool. Babe didn't tell me you were an actor, Roman. What's the show about?" he asked.

Roman smiled at me. "Knox, you're such a gentleman," he said. "I mean, I'm not an actor. But you don't need to be to *be*, you know what I mean?"

Knox looked confused. "Not really," he said.

"A lot of actors these days, especially the ones that come out of Los Angeles, aren't really actors. They're just interesting people. That's what people want these days. They want to watch people on TV that they can relate to, not stuffy actor types to whom they can't relate for shit."

"I guess I know what you're saying. Like Nicole Richie?"

"Exactly like Nicole Richie."

We all smiled in agreement that while Nicole Richie may seem to be a talentless hack, she's actually a chic, enterprising, bright powerhouse of style and humor.

"I used to despise Nicole," I shared, putting my cigarette out. I'd forgotten how I hated American Spirits; they tasted like rhubarb. "I had to shave my head once because of her. But we've moved past that phase of tomfoolery and shenanigans. I guess I can say I'm okay with her now. She's a succubus from hell, but she's chic and enterprising so it's fine."

Roman's massage was done and he hopped off the table. Ray folded it up and was gone before I could say "lace front."

"Anyway," said Roman, taking a seat at the table with us, "Babe tells me you're quite the chef. What have you got for us here?"

"I just made a quick, easy brunch from what you had in the kitchen. Which was actually a lot of really great and really expensive stuff. I hope you don't mind."

"It's fine. I don't use that room. Knock yourself out."

"Oh, I did. I actually Knoxed myself out."

I laughed so hard at his sweet, dumb joke that my eyelids started to hurt. It was like one of those moments when a parent is clearly too obsessed with their kid to even see clearly so they make a huge deal over the dumbest shit.

Once I'd recovered, Knox pointed at a clump of food on the plate.

"Here we've got a potato-and-onion frittata and some super yummy banana grain pancakes. . ."

The meal looked like a photo from one of those magazines about food that I've never really looked inside of, but could imagine. Roman was stunned. He gave me a look, then back to Knox, then back to me, Knox, me again.

"Why are you?" he finally asked Knox.

"Why am I?" Knox asked back.

"Yeah, like, why are you like this?"

"Um . . ."

Knox looked at me. I think he was intimidated by Roman, a gay marvel in his own right.

"I mean," Roman said, "how did you learn to cook like this? You're so young. I don't understand."

"I think it's insane, too," I added. "Everyone knows I was an extremely old and wise soul as a kid, blazing trails in both the fashion and art worlds, but this is next level. When I was ten I was still into people doing things for me, not doing things myself. Doing things is an immensely adult concept and cooking is *such* a do."

"I don't really know," answered Knox. "I got into it at first because my mom would ask me to cook for the three of us. Yeah, since I'm, like, five or six, she'd have me get dinner together. And I got sick of eating pizza and Chinese food. We don't have that many cute options around where I'm from."

"It's all so tragic," Roman said.

"But hopeful," I chimed in, putting a soft hand on Knox's shoulder.

The three of us ate brunch in silence. It was that good. I was officially someone who enjoyed food now. I knew it wasn't chic and that it went against everything I'd built for myself over the span of my preciously curated lifetime, but I ate for Knox. Oh, Roman and I got a little rosé-drunk, too.

Maybe *Everyone eats food or they die* is my mantra?

Next on my agenda was a quick jump over to Barneys Beverly Hills.

"Don't, like, buy me tons of shit, Babe. Really. I'll feel bad and my mom will super, crazy, totally freak out and make me sell it all and, like, give the money to charity."

"I won't. I promise. I mostly just need things for myself," I lied.

That afternoon, I ended up buying myself a really good Loewe basketweave tote, and for Knox: two pairs of Dolce & Gabbana wool pants, six Paul Smith shirts (three striped, two polka-dotted, one floral), a down Moncler jacket, a down Moncler vest, down Moncler pants, four Orlebar Brown polos that I thought would be great for school, adorable Stella McCartney "Days of the Week" briefs, a Y-3 baseball cap, a pair of Y-3 striped sweatpants, two pairs of Margiela Replica sneakers that were too big but he can grow into them, and a Vetements hoodie, which almost made Knox cry when he tried it on. They were born to be together. It was a dress on him, but we both liked it that way. Especially with the reflective Dior sunglasses I bought him but didn't list above because I love a fashion secret.

We were both beat to smithereens from the running around, pulling sizes, prancing in different looks, drinking sparkling water, and crying. So this outing obvs called for a nap after. But it was a power nap.

"Wake the fuck up. We're going out," I announced to the dark room in Roman's house where we were slumbering. Knox was still asleep on the bed next to me. It was 9 p.m.

"Babe. I'm ten years old. How many fucking times do I have to remind you that? I can't go out to clubs and stuff."

"First of all, you're not allowed to curse."

"You do it constantly."

"I know this, but it sounds weird coming out of your mouth. Give it a few months, you can say fuck and cunt and bitch and shit and pussy and cock when you're eleven, deal?"

"I don't get it. But fine, deal," Knox agreed.

"Okay, so what are we wearing tonight?"

"I don't know. I'm kinda tired. The audition is tomorrow."

"Of course the audition is tomorrow. You think I forgot the sole reason why I kidnapped you all the way out here?"

"So maybe I should just rest, then?"

"What?! Knox, you are in Los Angeles, the best slash worst city in the entire world, for basically just one night. You need to see more of it. Trust me, you'll be fine tomorrow. You'll be totes inspired by our night and you'll walk into that fucking audition with all of the charisma, uniqueness, nerve, and talent that it's gonna take to win. I promise. I'm your manager, okay? You have to trust me. Going out will only inspire you to get that spot on the show. You'll be lit like a glorious, burning torch. And it's not like you'll be hung over or anything."

"Okay."

"Okay?"

"Okay. What are we wearing?" he asked with a new hint of anticipation in his voice.

I thought on it for a second. I considered us going in a neohippie direction, then I mentally dressed us in complete Hood by Air looks replete with chains, ties, zippers, and cutouts. I took a contemplative sip of the Vitamin Water Zero on the nightstand, and finally it hit me.

"We're wearing Prada."

"Are you thinking what I'm thinking?" he asked. Knox looked at me like he was Pinky and I was the Brain.

"If you're thinking spring '11, then yes, I am thinking what you're thinking."

The two of us then erupted into what can only be described as pure romper room fuckery/shenanigans. Dancing on the bed, screaming, prancing around the house, and generally causing a raucous extravaganza of unadulterated fashion queerness. I broke a lamp. It looked Persian and expensive. Hehe.

We did each other's hair and makeup and, after a quick stop at my West Hollywood storage unit to pick up our looks, Knox and I were on our way to meet some friends for sushi at the SUGARFISH on La Brea for a rezzie at 10:30. We yassed the entire Uber ride there.

So here's the thing: I want to tell you that the night went totally smooth from this point on, but I can't do that because that'd be a lie. I actually can't tell you much about the night because as soon as we met Genevieve and a few other randoms that don't matter at sushi, I got blackout wasted. It was not what I'd call cute.

"Eat this!" I remember screaming at Knox and my friends whenever more fish would come, followed inevitably by an ear-piercing howl. Heads were turning, waiters were peacefully requesting our table to turn it down, it was a mess. But no fucks were given, clearly, because the photos from dinner are amazing and my hair was doing this thing it does sometimes where it looks blown out at the bottom but totally straight and tight at the top. It sounds crazy but trust me, it's a glorious occasion when it occurs and the cameras were living for it.

At some point one to four hours later, Knox and I, in our full electric, striped, tropical, twisty, monkey-printed Prada looks with bold feather boas, found ourselves in the back of Bar Marmont (they let me in with a minor because I'm me).

"No, *Superman Returns* was your best work. I swear to God! You were my favorite Lex Luthor in history. I almost want to tell you you could fuck me tonight, even though I know you wouldn't 'cause my dick's not big enough for you!"

Yep. That's right. I shouted that at Kevin Spacey.

Then my attention was drawn to my phone. It was a

missed call from Scott. Maryland Scott? OMG yes—the only other Scott I had in my phone was Scott Weiland, and I knew it couldn't have been him. Shit. This person had called me three times. It must've been morning in Maryland because it was already 3:30 in LA.

"Where's Knox?" I remember saying to Kevin. He'd just walked away at some point.

I decided in that moment that calling Scott would stress me out but was ultimately the right thing to do because he might be able to help me find Knox.

So I found a seat on some wet grass outside, lit a Marlboro Light, and called him back.

THIRTEEN

I'm fucking Smart.

"Hello? Babe?" Scott said through the phone. He sounded not drunk. Isn't it hilarious how, when you're wasted, you are hyperaware of how drunk or not drunk everyone else seems?

"Hello. You've reached Babe Walker's phone."

I sounded drunk.

"I know whose phone it is. I just called it. And you called me back."

"Scott?"

"Yeah, Babe."

"Oh my God, hey! What's up? It's Babe."

I wanted to sound as put together as possible.

"Jesus. Hey. Are you okay? It's super late there."

"I'm totally fine. Knox is fine. We're gonna be fine. We're out here making it in LA, okay?"

"Well, Veronica has been—"

"You can just relax. Tell Vee she needs to chill out. I've got this."

"You've got this?"

"Yas, queen. I've got this. Knox is gonna do great. I'm making his dreams come true."

"All right, well, his mom has been basically hysterical trying to figure out where you took him and what's going on out there. I know that Knox seems mature for his age and I think it's great that he's found someone that he looks up to, but you—"

"I bought him the CUTEST shit. You'll just die, Scott. I know you'll especially die for the Y-3 stuff we picked up at Barneys today because it's so sporty and you're sporty 'cause you're, like, a PE teacher or something, right?"

"I teach English but I also coach," Scott said flatly.

"Right, that's what I said. You're a coach. Not a teacher."

"Yeah, uh . . . no . . . but okay."

"Hey, Scott?"

"Babe. Can you tell me what you guys are doing right now? Where are you?"

"I think that's fucking hot. That you're a coach."

"Are you out at a bar?"

"Of course I'm at a fucking bar," I said, waving good-bye to Alexa Chung, who looked very thin and very amazing. She mouthed, "Call me" and was out of sight. Moments later, I could see a flurry of paparazzi flashes over the ivy-covered wall.

"Babe? You still there?" Scott demanded.

"I'm here, I'm here," I assured him, lighting another cigarette. "You really called me at, like, the worst time ever. I've been received by LA with such warmth tonight, after nearly a week away, so a lot of people are trying to talk to me and fuck me and be my friend. I should go. Big night for me."

"Where is Knox?!"

"He's right beer."

"Right *beer*? What?"

"HERE. He's right here. I'm looking at him," I lied.

"Okay. Good. That's good. We're super worried over here."

"There's nothing to worry about. I swear."

"Can I suggest something?" Scott asked.

"Can I not listen?"

"Sure. But for Knox's sake, I really think you should."

"Okay, fine."

That hit me hard. I was drunk, yes, but I could hear a true sense of worry in Scott's voice. He was afraid I might put Knoxers in a dangerous situation, which is NOT cute. The fact that I didn't know where Knox was started to really settle in. I was basically positive that he was still with Roman and my friends inside, in a corner, but the truth was, I had no idea.

"Can you find somewhere quieter to talk to me?" Scott asked.

"Yeah, give me literally one minute. I'll go inside."

"Okay, bring Knox with you. Don't leave him alone."

"Obviously. Come on, Knoxie," I said to no one.

The place was almost empty by this point in the night but the usual hangers-on were stomping about, eyes wide, swigging gin and tonics and looking for an after-hours party at the closest house with a gate. Gates make famous people feel okay with their drug habits. I was looking for Knox but also for a quiet corner where I could talk to Scott.

"Have you seen my short friend?" I asked the youngest Jenner girl—I can never remember her name—as she passed me, putting my hand over the phone so that Scott wouldn't hear me asking where Knox was. I figured she was also a child, so maybe she'd been hanging out with Knox or at least knew where I could find him.

"You mean that little boy you came in with?" the Jenner said.

"Yes! You know where he is?"

"No. He's super cute, though. He was showing us how to make origami before."

"Oh, cute! I mean, how cute is he?!"

"So cute," she agreed, emotionless.

"But you have no idea where he is?"

"None whatsoever," Jenner said. "Do you?" she asked her friend.

"Who?" said the friend, not looking up from her phone, hair covering her face. It totally might've been Caitlyn Jenner, but I was too wrapped up in the missing child case at hand to investigate further. But Caitlyn, if you're reading this, I love you and truly admire your choice to hire Jen Rade as your stylist—the white custom Versace dress at the ESPYs was a fashion moment I'll tell my future kids about.

"Forget it!" I shouted at them and stormed off into the bar.

I was getting proper nervous now.

"Scott?! Are you still there?" I said, stepping out into the hallway. "Okay, tell me what to do. I get it. I fucked up."

"Hey, I'm here. It's okay. If Knox is there with you then it's fine. But I want you guys to get on a plane to Baltimore first thing in the—"

"He's not here! OKAY!? I lied!" I said pathetically into the phone. "I fucking lost him! He's probably dead!!"

Then I felt a pull on the back of my jacket. I spun around so fast that I almost threw my phone across the room. It was little Knoxie. Thank Christ.

"Babe. What the actual fuck? You left me in there."

"Just kidding!" I said into the phone.

"You found him?" asked Scott.

"He's right here."

"Can you put him on the phone?"

"It's Scott, the coach from your school," I said, handing the phone to Knox. We both sat on the floor with our backs against the wall. My back was hurting from the bed at Roman's, and I was fucking exhausted from the drama of the previous twenty minutes. TBH, I needed another drink.

"Hey, Mr. Chapman . . . Yeah . . . I'm fine . . . It wasn't her fault . . . I was just wandering around on my own . . . I know . . . I know . . . Yeah, I understand . . . It's tomorrow . . . Really? . . . But . . . My mom said that? . . . Okay . . . Yeah, I know . . . Yeah, we did . . . Lots of Prada. Like, tons of Prada . . . I know, I'm kind of dying . . . Uh-huh . . . . Okay, I will . . . Yeah . . ."

Knox handed the phone back to me. He did look pretty wiped out.

"Hey, Scott, it's me."

"So here's what's gonna happen now. I need you to pay attention."

"I'm listening, I swear."

"Okay. There's a flight out of LA at 9:30 a.m. that I want you guys on."

"Scott, the *MasterChef Junior* audition is tomorrow. I'm obvs taking Knox to the audition. Don't be crazy."

He paused for a second. I heard a deep, pensive breath.

"You're a smart person, right, Babe?"

"Is this a test?"

"No."

"Yes, I'm fucking smart. Hello? You met me."

"Well, as a fellow smart person, I'd like to acknowledge the fact that sometimes we do things because our heart tells us to, not because they are actually smart decisions. Do you know what I mean when I say that?"

"Please don't patronize me. I'm wasted and did a little bit more MDMA tonight than I had originally wanted to, but I'm not a child. So you don't need to speak to me like I am."

"Babe, you literally kidnapped someone else's child, an individual for whom you have no guardian's rights, no legal papers stating that you're his caretaker, nothing."

"You clearly don't understand the bond that's been born

between Knox and myself," I said, winking at Knox who was now leaning on my shoulder and starting to doze off.

"What you're doing is illegal, and the sentence for kidnapping in this country can be anywhere between fifteen years to life in prison. Do you like prison movies?"

The world stopped in this moment. I thought about Scott's question for a while. So long, in fact, that he started just shouting my name over and over until I finally said something.

"We'll come back tomorrow."

"Thank you."

"As long as there are seats left in first class."

Scott laughed. He had the best laugh, very masc, very sexy. And that meant he didn't hate me.

"There are. I already checked because I knew you'd ask."

"Oh, okay, that's creepy slash amazing. Are you my husband, Scott? Seriously, I feel like we have a super deep—"

"Get some sleep. You're doing the right thing. Now get a cab and go home."

"We are, we are. I'm hanging up."

"Okay. I'll call Veronica now and let her know that you guys are coming back in the morning."

I was about to hit the "end" button on my phone but I pulled it back up to my ear. "You still there?"

"Yeah, what's up?" he said.

"Nothing. Just . . . thanks for looking out for Knox."

"Oh, yeah, sure thing. I love that fuckin' kid."

I hung up. A single tear. Without even trying.

Knoxie and I literally ran the fuck out of the hotel, no good-byes. We hopped into a cab, and I told the driver the address to my dad's house. I knew Roman's place would still be a party at this hour.

"We're going to your house?" Knox asked, watching the city pass us through the window.

"Yeah, it just makes more sense. I'll schedule for a messenger to bring all of our shit over, so don't worry about that. And I already organized shipment of your Barneys stuff to your house."

"Okay."

I felt guilt. I hate feeling guilt. But I'd let my wonderful, vulnerable new love down tonight. I was supposed to be a role model, not get sloshed and lose him at the Chateau.

"You okay?" I asked quietly, unsure if he'd fallen asleep.

"I'm okay. It was fun. Just a lot of people. I didn't know what to do or say. I normally know what to say to people. Tonight I felt, like, weird about myself."

"That has nothing to do with you. It's just LA. It can make people feel bad about themselves."

"Don't get me wrong," he said, adjusting in his seat to face me. "I still think I'm fierce. LA won't change that."

"Yes!!" I shouted. The cabdriver gasped.

By the time we got to my house, it was almost 4:30 a.m. Knox climbed out of the cab and stood in the driveway looking at the property.

"I almost can't believe I'm really here."

"It's gorge, right?" I said, handing a hundred-dollar bill to the driver and telling him to drive away quietly. I really didn't want to wake Mabinty because she has a gun.

"It's so gorge. It's, like, insane that you grew up here."

"It's not that weird. Get over it."

"Let me just enjoy this moment, okay?"

"You're a freak, and I love you."

"You're a way bigger freak, Babe. Like, the biggest freak I've basically ever met. You break every rule ever and . . ."

"What?"

"I'm glad we came, even if it all didn't work out with the show."

"Don't worry about that right now. I'm so fucking tired. Let's go inside."

We walked over to the guesthouse, and I showed him to a room he could sleep in. He was right about this house.

It's amazing, the history between these walls. SO many chic moments, so many tragic moments, an old fuck-buddy even died here. Remember that mess? Just so much fucking Babe Walker life force everywhere. I was glad Knox was here to enjoy some of that.

I couldn't sleep because I was still fucked up. So I texted my dad.

Babe Dad

Dad Babe

Babe Where are you

Dad Berlin

Dad Julianne is being honored at a film festival here and there's a big party for her so she invited Lizbeth and I

Babe Moore?

Dad Yes darling

Babe Chic

Dad What are you doing up? You're in LA, yes? Isn't it 5 in the morning there

Babe Yes. Long story. I'm here with Knox. We're at the house.

Babe it's really nice to be home

Babe I missed it here. I miss you.

Dad I miss you madly darling. How's it going with the Donna of it all

Babe Oh she's such a bitch. But I love Knox

Babe I'm so excited for you to meet him

Dad I'd like that

Dad Any developments on the paternity front?

Babe I mean

Babe I'm pretty much positive that he's my brother. We're just too similar to be merely kin. He's a miniBabe

Dad Sounds frightful

Babe Oh fuck off dad

Dad You know I'm only joking darling

Babe Sure

Babe :)

Babe I kinda fucked up tonight though dad

Dad Tell me darling. I'm all ears. Just here in the room waiting for Lizbeth to finish dressing. We're going to a few museums today before the event tonight

Babe Boring

Dad You know she likes museums. I couldn't give less of a shit about museums.

Dad But she likes them.

Dad So, we'll go for a few hours.

Babe You're sweet

Dad I've been trying

Babe So earlier tonight I got really drunk and lost Knox at The

Chateau and this boy I like from Maryland called me to tell me I was irresponsible and he basically attacked me, dad, and I felt so stupid because the last thing I want to do is fuck up Knoxie AT ALL. He's so presh.

Dad What? Where is he now?? Tell me you found him.

Babe Yes duh

Babe I'm not a complete moron. Jesus.

Dad Good. You could go to jail Babe. You don't want to go to jail.

Dad You do have his mother's permission to have him in LA don't you darling?

Babe Yeah basically

Dad What do you mean basically

Babe It's fine dad. I'm taking him back to Maryland in a few hours and life will resume to normal, boringness

Babe The adventure is over

Babe It's fine. I'm fine.

Dad Are you sure darling?

Babe Yeah

Dad Is there anything else you wanted to tell me?

Babe Actually yeah. while I have you, I want to get your opinion on a purchase I've been mulling over.

Dad I'm not buying you a baby elephant. Baby elephants grow to full grown elephants, you know that right? Besides, you're hardly at the house anymore. It would go neglected. The whole bloody thing would be a stich up, and while I appreciate that you're going after what you want in life, this is just a battle you're going to lose, love.

Babe Relax

Babe I'm not gonna ask you to buy a baby elephant again.

Dad Thank god. What is it then?

Babe I'm thinking of buying myself a plane.

Dad With what money?

Babe Not worrying about that yet. But hear me out. I'm basically becoming Knox's big sister/mentor/sherpa/personal shopper and for him to flourish the way he deserves to, he's going to need to be meeting with me at least once quarterly, if not monthly. This is a big turning point moment in his life and he just needs someone like me there by his side making sure that he stays chic and major and good. Remember how malleable and spongelike I was when I was ten?

Dad Of course I remember. I remember taking you to see Hole and praying that you wouldn't start idolizing Courtney Love.

Babe But I do idolize Courtney Love. Less now in light of recent accusations that she may have been involved in a con-spiracy to kill Kurt, but I'm not emotionally stable enough to get into that at the moment.

Dad I think she did it.

Babe Don't say that, Dad.

Dad Darling, she is a hoodlum. That's why you love her.

Babe God damnit, you're always right. Anyway, what do you think of my Babe Airways idea?

Dad I think it's ridiculous.

Babe Really?

Dad I think if your bond with this lad is as strong as you say it is, you'll find a way to stay in his life.

Babe I'm happy you're happy but I'm sad that you're not gonna buy me a plane for becoming a better person over the last week.

Dad Absolutely not.

Babe Fine

Dad I'm proud of you Babe. I know you may have fucked up a wee bit by bringing him out to LA but I know your heart was in the right place, that's my girl.

Babe Thanks Dad

Babe That means a lot

Babe I'm crying

Dad Don't cry darling

Babe I'm not really.

Babe I thought you might change your mind about the plane if you thought I was that emotionally invested but it's whatever.

Dad I respect that you tried.

Babe Thanks

Babe Okay. I should try to sleep for like five minutes before we have to catch our flight. I'm fucking exhausted and hungover already and just need to namaste for a moment. I love you

Dad I love you more.

Babe Oh and tell Lizbeth that I'm still working on my mantra. I know she doubted me

Dad She never doubted you, darling. She only wants what's best for you. She wants you to find your path and do it with pride and strength

Babe EEEWWWWWW

Babe You sound like her

Dad You're right

Dad I've been with the woman for a few days straight. And don't get me wrong, she's lovely, but I don't want to sound like a yoga teacher.

Dad Thanks for always being honest with me.

Dad Keep your head up, darling. You know I love you.

Babe Love you too.

Babe Just for shits, what is she wearing to the event?

Dad Let me ask her

Dad She says she's wearing a strapless Zac Posin

Babe It's Posen and ew.

Babe Tell her I said ew.

Babe Did you tell her?

Dad Obviously I'm not going to tell her that. It's a beautiful dress. She bought it last week.

Babe You guys literally make me vom. Love you both.

Dad Ciao darling

Babe X

FOURTEEN

Alex Trebek's Dick (and Also His Balls).

As I sat in my kitchen, making myself some delicious boiling water with lemon zest (one of my all-time fave comfort foods and a go-to LA breakfast), I realized how very strange I felt. Not because it had been so long since I'd been at my dad's, but more because I woke up thinking about someone other than myself. Normally the first thought I have when I realize I'm awake has to do with what smoothie I'm going to have, or what I'm going to pick for my first look of the day, or how many people will ask me if I'm a model that day. That's just who I am, and I'm okay with it.

But this morning was different. I was obvi tired because I'd only slept for about 4.2 hours and they were drunk hours, but when I woke up, I was thinking about Knox. Not about *what we were going to do today on our flight* or *if he was going to compliment my plane outfit*. But more general thoughts about how he was and how he slept and if he was okay. This mom thing that was happening to me was getting out of hand.

Babe Hey. How'd you sleep?

Knox Still sleeping

Babe Me too but we need to be in the car in 1 hour to make this flight

Knox k

Babe Pack

Knox kk

I kept thinking about what Scott had said. And all the texts from Vee. She must have been really worried about Knox. The gravity of me "kidnapping" Knox was starting to become clear. I mean, I was sober enough last night to book us the flight back to Maryland when I got back to our house, but I was too drunk to really grasp the emotional severity of it all. By bringing Knox to LA for this audition, I was just doing what I thought was best for him. I wanted him to have every opportunity to be happy, but I honestly didn't think anyone would really care that I stole him for a few days. No one in Maryland seemed to really pay attention to what he was up to anyway, so I was halfway convinced that Veronica and Cara wouldn't even know Knox was gone. I thought Kris Jennering him was the right move. I guess I was wrong.

I looked at my phone, checking/hoping our flight was delayed. I could have used an extra few hours of sleep and a few more hours of not dealing with whatever was waiting for me when I got off that plane. Also, they only had business class available by the time I booked, so I was not looking forward to that noise. You may think I'm a monster, but I really, really, really prefer first class.

There would be other auditions for *MasterChef Junior*. Veronica could take him to one of those. I needed to get him back to Maryland.

"MABINTY!!!!"

I waited for a response, staring out at space. Nothing.

"MAAAAAAAAAAAAAAAAAAAAAAAAAABS!!!!!"

I hadn't seen her when I got to the house because it was basically dawn. But she was most likely in the house. I needed her advice. She knew me best and I could talk to her about everything. I mean, she'd raised me. She was my mom, for all intents and purposes.

Babe Mabs where the fuck r u

Mabinty Can't talk. Busy.

Babe I'm in LA. I'm in my room. Come hither.

Mabinty No.

Babe Stop

I got up, pulled my hair into the chicest and highest of ponies, brushed my teeth, peed, took a huge shit. LOL. Can you imagine if I was being serious? I've literally never taken a huge shit in my life. That would be fucking sick. I realized it was 7:05 a.m. so I marched my tired, hungover ass out of the guesthouse (my house) and down to the laundry room, which is in the basement of my dad's house.

BTW/FYI/ALSO: Mabs smokes weed every day for breakfast at 7 a.m. while watching the previous day's episode of *Jeopardy!* She is in LOVE with Alex Trebek. She has been dreaming about fucking him since she met him at my dad's office Christmas party in 2001 and he told her that she had beautiful eyes.

To my surprise, when I finally reached the laundry room (my dad's house is really big and sometimes I get lost), Mabinty was not in there. So weird. She is always, always, always in there at this time of the morning. I'm rarely up this early, but sometimes when I come back from a night out, she is already in there hitting her blunt. Love that for her. But where was she now? Maybe she slept out of the house? She didn't know I was going to pop in. Maybe Carl (her on-again-off-again BF) called her for a booty call? Good for her.

So I went back upstairs to the kitchen, finished my boiling water with lemon zest, and headed back up to my room to pack. I had to choose a few key looks that said *I'm sorry for kidnapping your son but I'm more sorry that I might be the first person in his life to take his dreams seriously.*

As I passed by the guest room that Knox was staying in, I knocked on the door. There was no answer, but it sounded like the water was running, so he was probably taking a shower. He is so cute.

I continued on to my room, quickly showered, put on "plane" makeup, which is similar to gym makeup, which is similar to therapy makeup, and threw on a baby-blue stretch linen blazer that I'd forgotten I bought at Acne before I left for Maryland and some amazing jeans from The Row. Punctuating the look with my white Raf Simons Stan Smiths. I contemplated a black patent Valentino pump, but then remembered we were flying commercial. Only wear heels if you're flying private. That's an actual rule.

As I brushed my teeth, I looked at myself in the mirror. For someone who was completely hungover and deprived of sleep, I looked gorgeous. There was a new kind of confidence I was noticing in myself in the last few days. I'm generally a very confident person, but there was something different about this. It was less cunt-fidence and more just regular-person *I can do it I'm worthy and so blessed* confidence. Actual happiness? Maybe.

I quickly zipped up my two massive pieces of Goyard luggage that I'd never unpacked from my last trip to Maryland. I got my two suitcases downstairs and to the front door, where I saw that Knox had left his shit.

I walked out to the Uber that was waiting for me in our driveway. His name was Robert, which made me experience a weird energy for about thirty seconds.

"Hi. Thanks for waiting. Can you help me with some luggage?" I said as I got into the backseat of the black Yukon. This Robert and my Robert were very different. Driver Robert was midfifties, ethnically ambiguous, and about five foot one.

"Are you Babe Walker?"

"I am. I'm so flattered that you recognized me. Kind of embarrassing, actually. So early for me. How'd you recognize me? Did you read my books, or do you know my work on social media, or were you there that time at

Nobu Malibu when I threw a glass of hot sake at Brody Jenner?"

"I'm just asking if you're the person who ordered this Uber. They make us verbally verify that you are the person who ordered the car. It's company policy. Also the picture in your Uber profile is of the back of someone's head. So I honestly wasn't sure if you were her."

"Got it. Totally makes sense. But just so you know, you wouldn't have been the first Uber driver I've had who was also a fan of my work."

"Okay, miss."

"We are still waiting on one more passenger."

"Sounds good. I'll go grab the luggage now?"

"Yeah, it's just inside the front door there."

Robert loaded up the car. I checked Instagram—it was boring as fuck, per usual. We waited for Knox.

Then we waited some more. Where was he? He was obviously dressed because his suitcase was already packed.

Babe ?

Babe you coming? We gotta go

I decided to give him five more minutes. Nothing makes me more edgy than being rushed. Especially on a travel day. I decided to write a poem while I waited.

Robert The Second

There are other Robert's in my life now.
And I

Okay, time's up. Where in the fuck is Knox? I had a look to the back of the SUV to make sure he grabbed everything and, after counting the bags twice, I noticed that one of Knox's bags wasn't there. Only his clothes suitcases were there. Where was that chic little knife bag I'd bought him at that godforsaken mall? He usually rests it on top of his rolling bag. At least that's what he'd done on the way out here. FUCK!!!

"Robert, I'm sorry, did you notice anyone leaving this house before I came out?"

"I didn't."

"Okay, then I'm confused. I need to go back into the house for a few and find my cousin slash brother slash travel partner slash Knox."

"Sure. Take your time. I did see a black Mercedes sedan pulling out of the gate when I was pulling in."

"Goddammit! Did you happen to notice anyone in the passenger seat of the car?"

"Yeah. A kid, I think?"

"Fucking Mabinty. I can't believe these stunt queens."

I took out my phone and called her.

"Ya?"

"Mabinty Jones, what on earth do you think you're doing?"

"Mi tyook ya boy to his damn audition. Ya know dat boy got real talent, gyal? Besides, dat lil' cutie wouldn't shut de fuck up 'bout it. Mi had to do da right ting."

"Yes, Mabs, of course I know he has talent. But—"

"He made me a crepe this morning from scratch. Tryna convince me to take his scrawny ass down to the Fox lot. Dis boy has crepe skills."

"How dare you kidnap my relative? He'd already been kidnapped by me. You can't double-kidnap a ten-year-old. It's completely unethical."

"Well, he just got tru di first round and now they movin' him upstairs."

"What!? Oh my God! Yes!! Go Knox!" I shouted into the phone. "I'm so proud of him!"

"Mi too. Mi too, gyal."

"I'll be there in thirty."

I sat there for a second.

"Robert. Change of plans. We're going to Century City. I'll put the address into the app."

"Roger that, Miss Walker."

Ew.

FIFTEEN

The Most Expensive Uber Ride of My Life.

As I opened the door to the dark stage and the cold air rushed toward me, I realized how nervous I was. This was huge for Knox. I knew how talented he was and how much he wanted this. It was like all of my hopes and dreams somehow transferred over to him in that moment and all I wanted was what he wanted. I told the driver Robert to wait. I needed him standing by in case Knox didn't make it to the next round and I had to get him out of there quickly. I would be such an incredible stage mom. I was *being* such an incredible stage mom.

"Let's give a warm *MasterChef Junior* welcome to the

one, the only, Chef Gordon Ramsay!" a woman with a microphone yelled.

Holy. Fuck. I forgot that this was Gordon's show. My dad has represented him for years. They came up in London together. Gordon is actually so fucking hot. I know you've never come to this conclusion on your own, but it's true, and I'm always happy to be the one to tell you what you actually think. Maybe it's all the screaming that he does, or maybe it's his weird face and rough hands, but the atmosphere he creates around himself is exhilarating to be around. Not my normal type of guy, but definitely very fuckable. Gordon walked out onto the soundstage and took the microphone as the crowd of quaint little children dressed in those chef robes and their parents exploded in applause.

"Thank you, thank you. Thrilled to be back for another season of *MasterChef Junior*," Gordon began. He really seemed to mean it. "If you're in this room, it means you are one of the top one hundred chefs between the age of eight and thirteen in America!"

The crowd went nuts. I caught a glimpse of Knox and Mabinty in the last row of the bleachers and headed right toward them.

"You've all been selected to be in this group of one hundred because our judges see something special in each and everyone of you. By the end of today, we will have selected our final twenty-four chefs for the televised portion of our program. But first you will be put through two more rounds of auditions to determine who our contestants will be. So I will ask that all the boys please line up over to my left and check in with Janet over here . . . and all the young ladies please line up to my right and check in with Kelly. You should all be very proud of making it this far. I hope to see you soon on the program. Best of luck, chefs!"

And with that, Gordon was out of there. Who knew he had it in him to be so kind and loving to other human beings? Me. I knew. I waited for Knox and Mabs at the bottom of the stairs because I avoid stairs when I can. They're an involuntary StairMaster, and I'm not working on my ass right now, so no thanks. Knox saw me, and his eyes lit up. He hopped over a bunch of rows and pushed through a gaggle of losers (mini-chefs) to get to me. He literally jumped into my arms, and I held him up. He was light. Or I was strong? Or it's true what they say about developing superhuman strength in moments of extreme concentration.

"Babe, it was amazing! I was, like, totally in the zone and they asked me to make an egg-white omelette, and I'm, like, amazing at omelets because it's my mom's favorite breakfast. SO . . . I was like, duh? And I caramelized these mushrooms that they had with a little bit of white wine, and the judge told me it was the first time any kid had thought to caramelize mushrooms at an audition, and it was maybe the best omelet she had ever tasted and I'm really, really sorry that I left you at the house, but I just had to come here. I could feel it in my bones that I had to be here. I feel bad but also not bad. Are you mad? Please don't be mad at me. I just wanted to finish what we started."

I was taken aback. Knox was holding on to me for dear life. I don't think I've ever caught someone before.

"Knox. It's okay," I said as I held on to him. "I get it. Congratulations. I'm so proud of you."

"You're not mad?"

"NO!" I shouted, overcome. "What?! You rose from the ashes of my irresponsibility like the fucking PHOENIX THAT YOU ARE and I could NOT be more proud!"

I felt the eyes of a few parents on my back. *Yes, I said fucking, get off me.*

"Boy. Mi promise yuh, there ain't no chance dat dis gyal would be able to be mad at yuh after how good yuh dun today," Mabinty added.

"Did you leave the water running to make it seem like you were showering in your room? Because if so, that was brilliant. I was completely fooled. So something I'd do, so well done."

Knox honestly looked like he was going to explode with happiness. I hadn't seen anyone smile that big since Genevieve found out snorting Cialis could make her nipples hard.

"I need to go line up over with the rest of the boys who made it this far. I overheard someone saying that the next round is all about chopping and mincing, which is supes cute because I've been really focusing on both of those skills in the last few months."

"Ya gwan crush it, mi little love," Mabinty told him. She was in this, too. The three of us were such a chic, multicultural family, and I was dying for us.

"I'm sure that you're going to do great. Just breathe and remember that you are a better chef than all of these other pieces of shit."

"Thanks for the vote of confidence, Babe. But I saw this thirteen-year-old girl preparing a coq au vin that would blow your mind."

"I'm gonna take your word for it. You better get over there and line up."

Mabinty and I each gave Knox a hug and he joined the rest of the group.

"In some ways, this kid and I are so similar. But when I was ten, I would have never had the kind of drive and focus," I said to Mabinty as we walked with the rest of the parents into a large room that had coffee and pastries.

"Yuh must be trippin', gyal. When yuh was a little one yuh drove mi crazy with all yuh drive and focus. Not one day went by without yuh bahderin' mi wit yuh practicin' yuh fashion and yuh stylin' clothes et cetera . . ."

"Really?"

"Every day ina di week began wit yuh pickin' out yuh outfits and yuh dresses and then changin' dem outfits tree hundred times before settlin' ona di one yuh liked most of all."

"I mean, I kind of remember that. But it's not the same as what Knox does. He, like, practices chopping shit. He works hard at it."

"And so did mi little Babe. It's the same, gyal. That boy is related to yuh. No doubt in mi damn mind 'bout that."

I knew I had to talk to Mabinty about the Knox maternity issue.

"About that . . ."

"Mi already know."

"What do you mean?"

"Mi already know what yuh 'bout to tell mi. Concernin' dis little chef."

"What exactly do you think I'm going to say?"

"That Knox not yuh cousin, he's yuh bruddah."

"What the fuck, Mabinty? You knew?"

"As soon as mi met him dis mornin', mi knew it."

"Just from meeting him? I don't get it. Are we that much alike? He could just be my cousin. I don't have any real proof. But I just met my grandfather, Joe, or whatever, and he said some intense shit about Knox being my brother. Fuck. Veronica. She's going to legit slice my throat when she sees me. Am I losing it?"

"He is yuh bruddah. One hundred percent."

"You knew? This whole time? How could you keep this from me?"

"Mi didn't know fuh sure until dis mornin'. Yuh see, mi saw Mrs. Donna at a gas station on Beverly Glen, back when yuh were in high school. Or at least mi thought mi saw her. She looked pregnant. Mi couldn't believe mi eyes. Mi wasn't sure it was her. How could mi bring it up to yuh or yuh father?"

"Jesus."

"Sorry, Babe." She was feeling for me. She cared. Love my Mabs.

I honestly felt like I'd been punched in the stomach. Not because I was shocked that this was the truth. But because I could actually imagine Donna, as a mom, pregnant as fuck, filling up her car in LA, when I was probably, like, two miles away, in high school, having no idea who the fuck/where the fuck my mom was. It all made me feel weird. It all made me fucking hate Donna. What a fucking cunt. Like, I already knew she was a cunt, but, like, what a fucking cunt.

"What a fucking CUNT!" I yelled a bit too loudly for the green room at *MasterChef Junior*, but I'd already established myself as the "young, hip parent" of the group so it was fine.

"Mi know dat's right, mi know. But now yuh have dis bruddah. And yuh can take care of dat boy. Sounds to mi like he got lucky wit yuh aunty takin' a care of him."

I gave it all a second's thought.

"Yeah. You're right. He is lucky. He's lucky he has me. My dad is gonna shit a brick when he finds out, though."

"Maybe, but the boy gonna shit an even bigga one."

"Yup. He sure is. Fuck. I don't know if I should tell him."

"What yuh need to do is tell yuh aunty that yuh know the truth. See what she say to yuh 'bout it. She da one dat's gotta deal wit dis. She raised him from da time he was a baby."

FULL. BLOWN. PANIC. ATTACK.

I don't know what triggered it, exactly, but it was happening. I popped the two Klonopin I'd been saving for the plane and just sat in that room with all of those other parents and guardians, looking at all of their weird bodies and faces. I couldn't have imagined a stranger, more awkward place to have confirmed my suspicions. The ramblings of

an elderly stranger were one thing; Mabinty's confidence
was another. I was in a daze. Everything seemed to be moving in slow motion, yet I had a feeling that in reality time
was passing very quickly. I remember Mabinty telling me
at one point that Knox had advanced to the final round. I
also remember talking to Veronica for a second and then
handing the phone to Mabinty, who I believe filled her in
on what was happening and why we were not going to land
on time.

I needed to snap the fuck out of my daze. It was not a
good look for me. Also, my brother was about to have one
of the happiest moments of his life or the darkest moments
of his life. He was going to need me either way. I was in no
shape to deal with him in my current state. I mustered up
enough energy to mouth the words "Diet Coke" to Mabinty
who kindly rushed over to the food table and grabbed me a
few diet beverages. I drank the most amount of Diet Coke
that I've ever had in one sitting. It really helped me. Like,
it actually helped me a lot. Thank you, kind people at Diet
Coke. You saved me.

"What time is it?" I asked Mabinty.

"One thirty."

"What? Are you serious? Did I fall asleep or something?"

"Mi don't know what yuh were doin' but Knox is about
to com thru dem doors. Yuh gonna be okay, gyal?"

"Yeah, I'm gonna be fine."

"Dat's right. Yuh Babe fuckin' Walker. Yuh can do what-eva yuh want. Also, mi rebooked yuh onto the red-eye flight. Yuh takin' off at nine thirty p.m. Veronica wants dat boy back. She no playin' around."

"Did they have first class? Please tell me they had first? I honestly cannot deal with business right now."

"Yuh in first class."

"Thank God. I don't think I would have survived a blow like that at this point in time."

The doors flew open, and bunch of kids filed into the room. Some of them had tears in their eyes. Some of them had their heads hanging low, facing the ground. This was clearly the group that didn't make the cut. I was praying that we wouldn't see Knox.

"Do you see him?" I asked Mabinty.

"Mi no see him."

"That's a good thing."

"Mi know."

All of the crying kids filed out with their parents, leaving us with all of the remaining parents, whose kids hadn't been released yet. I tried to do a quick count to see if I could get a sense of how many kids might be left inside the soundstage, but it was too hard to do mental math on Klonopin. Some of these families literally came with, like, twenty-seven people to support their little chef. Cute but relax.

We all waited in silence for what felt like an eternity. I was frantic, but I had a good feeling about it. I hadn't seen Mabinty look this unnerved since the time she got pulled over with an ounce of medical marijuana, which we had purchased for Coachella one year, in the backseat of her car. We weren't arrested, but they did take the weed from us so we just drove back home. There was no point. Finally, with a huge smile on his face, Knox came strolling through the door.

"I made it!"

I gave him a big hug and tears started streaming down my face as we embraced.

"I love you," I blurted out. I had no control over what had come out of my mouth.

"I love you too," Knox replied. He said it like we'd been saying it to each other our whole lives.

"We need to get to the airport. I have the Uber driver waiting outside for us. We are flying tonight. You can catch me up on everything on the way. K?"

"K."

We dropped Mabinty back at her car and then took the Uber to LAX. It was the most expensive Uber ride of my life ($1,194). Perhaps of anyone's life. I was proud.

SIXTEEN

Love Wins!

"Can I ask you a question?" Knox said.

We'd settled into our seats and reached cruising altitude or whatever the fuck that place in the air is where they start to let you drink. I was leafing through my crisp copy of the new *CR Fashion Book*, which had been waiting for me at my house in LA.

"Of course. Anything," I said, hoping it would be a yes-or-no and not something that involved opinion generating. I loved him but I was in magazine mode, not chat mode.

"Have you ever really, really liked someone? Or, like,

been in love? I know about Robert 'cause you put him in the book. Were you guys in love for real?"

Even I can't believe I'm saying this, but the fashion on my lap was going to have to wait. I gently closed the magazine and placed it in the seat-back pocket in front of me.

"Fuck yes, I've been in love," I started. "I've been in several different types of love."

"There are different types?"

"Oh, one hundred percent. I've been in love so many times, I can barely remember all of them. I've hated way more than I've loved, but still. There's been a lot of love."

"What do you mean?"

"I hate most things."

"Oh, no, I wanted clarification on the 'different' types of love."

"In my opinion, the most coveted love, the type of shit that makes you so happy that you're actually just sad, is the love I have for shoes. It's always been like this for me. Since I can remember, my devotion to good shoes has been so extreme, expensive, and all-consuming that it trumps my love for actual humans."

"I get it," Knox said.

"I know you do."

"You'll probably think this is basic, but when I bought

my first pair of Doc Martens, it meant the literal world to me. It was a long time ago—I was seven."

"Oh, so fifteen minutes ago?"

"Relax. You know I'm ten."

"I know, I know. Go on," I said through a laugh.

"They were black but, like, brushed with a silver paint and instead of laces they just had one zipper going up the front. Before I wore them out even once, I slept with them in bed with me. It sounds so dumb. I'd hold them in my arms as I fell asleep, and when I woke up I'd just stare at them. I even brought them to school as my show-and-tell item for the week when our class's unit was 'Pets.' Some fat kids made fun of me but my teacher said she understood why the shoes were like a pet to me. She, like, told the class that a pet is anything you love and want to take care of. I think she was just trying to make me feel better because of the bullying, but it didn't matter. I wanted those shoes so bad. And I loved them. And I wanted the world for them. My mom drove me to Baltimore to get them at this punk-rock store that smelled like the inside of one of our babysitters' car. She has a half-shaved head despite the fact that every time she babysits for us I tell her to shave the rest because it would be much better, much more editorial. She once asked me what 'editorial' meant. I told her to Google it, and she just laughed. It was sad, actually, 'cause I know she never

Googled it. She keeps her hair that way. Anyway, when I tried the boots on at the store, a feeling I'd never felt came over me. In my seven years, I'd never felt so connected to something. It was like the shoes were listening to me. Like they had been looking for me for years and they found their way to me. It was more of a reunion—"

"Than a meeting," I said, on the verge of tears.

"Yeah. It was like that. Ya know?"

"I know, Knoxie. I know," I said, full-blown crying.

"Stop crying, Babe. What the fuck?"

"It's just fucking emotional, okay?? You *have* been in love before. Love has no age limit. Love has no bounds! Love is love!" I shouted.

"Oh my God," Knox said, putting his hand over his face. I was embarrassing him.

"Sorry," I whispered. "I'm fine. I swear. No more shouting. No more crying."

I wiped my tears and got my shit together as fast as I could. Honestly, if it was possible to literally eat Knox in that moment, I would have. That's how much I loved him.

"Okay. So . . ." I said, composure basically regained.

"Besides your love for shoes and clothes, what about with, like, your boyfriends?"

"I was in love with Robert, of course I was. But it turned me into a monster. You know all about Babette. She's a succubus, a demon, a gargoyle with no God whatsoever. So I have to ask myself: Was that real love? Or was that something else? I think it's possession. I was possessed by the spirit my feelings for Robert elicited."

"You think if someone makes you crazy then you don't really like them?" Knox asked.

"No. I definitely liked Robert. But it was an unhealthy love for me. Even though I buried Babette a long time ago, there were still remnants of her bullshit antics living in me, and I knew they would until I broke up with Robert . . . again."

"I guess I get it."

"I have a question."

"All right."

"My question is: Why do you want to know?"

Knox took a gulp of the cranberry juice and seltzer mocktail that he'd mixed himself on his little pullout tray. He was literally always cooking. Then he looked at me, then away.

"I don't know," he said. "I was just wondering, I guess."

"Don't bullshit me."

"I'm not!"

"But, like, you are."

"I hate you," he said, smiling enough to let me know that he didn't actually.

"But, like, you love me."

"Ugh."

"What's wrong, muffin?"

I hated that I called him "muffin," but it came out and there was nothing I could do about it. Knox was not a muffin. If anything, Knox was a hemp seed and wheat berry biscuit from Cafe Clover on Downing Street in the West Village, but he knew that.

"Babe, this is hard."

"Are you gonna throw up? You kinda look like you're gonna throw up."

"No."

"You must have so many nerves from the day. The whole trip, actually. This is a lot for a child. You're still a child, Knox. Okay? It's okay if you need to throw up. Kids are allowed to throw up. I think. That's, like, a thing that can happen in public, and people are fine with it. Until they go through puberty. I mean, I'll hate you for doing it for a couple of seconds, but it's fine if you have to."

"I don't need to vomit!" he said with a mix of anger and frustration. It was like watching a mini-man aka a child actor.

"Okay. You don't need to vomit, that's good."

"There's something . . ."

"That you want to tell me?"

"Right. Yeah. There's something I want to, like, talk to you about but it's weird, I think."

His gaze was now fixed aggressively to his feet, to the floor. There was no way he was going to make eye contact with me. I gave him a few seconds, but he wasn't saying anything. This was super weird behavior for him, and I didn't exactly know how to respond to it.

"Knox," I said in a kind whisper. "When I was at rehab, a girl told me that her greatest fantasy in life was to transform herself with plastic surgery into an actual dolphin and then have sex with Rob Lowe. As in, she'd be a dolphin in dolphin form and Rob Lowe would be Rob Lowe in human form and they're banging and that's her fantasy. And to be totally honest, I wasn't fazed by it. I respected her candor. That's what she wanted and she had every right to be open about it. She's a free bitch just like you're a free bitch. You can talk to me, babes."

Please note: What *actually* happened when Jordana Connor confided in me about her Rob Lowe dolphin thing was this: I laughed extremely loud in her face, lit a cigarette, looked at her for a long time, shook my head, laughed more, and told literally everyone I talked to for the rest of my stay in Utah at that rehab facility.

Knox finally looked up at me.

"Who's Rob Lowe?"

"He's a friend of my dad's and played the plastic surgeon in *Behind The Candelabra*. You'll learn about him in your studies. Whatever. It doesn't matter who he is, that's not the point."

"I'm confused," Knox admitted. He looked it. I took a sip of my wine. I could obviously tell where this was going, and I was doing my best to lead him gracefully into the inevitable but I was only fucking him up. Was I gonna be a bad first person to come out to? A wave of literal terror shot from my toes upward. At the same moment the plane dipped for a second and the combo of it all caused me to scream, "OW!" which was embarrassing but just for a minute. Sometimes I say "ow" when I think I might get hurt but haven't been yet. I came back to Knox. This was his moment, not mine.

"Jesus fucking Christ, this plane. Okay. You know what, hold on," I said, throwing one finger in the air as uncuntily as possible. "Sorry, babes. I'll be right back."

I unclipped my seat belt, put my glass of wine on Knox's tray table, told him not to drink any of it, and walked over to the bathroom.

With the door locked behind me I took my hair out of the high pony, shook it out, and gave myself a long, focused look at my, um, self. I simply needed to take a breather to reflect and collect. Maybe that's my mantra?

Reflect . . . collect . . . reflect . . . collect . . .

No, that's fucking annoying. Anyway. I was in the middle of a crazy important moment in this boy's life, and it was just now hitting me like a ton of emotional bricks. If he was about to come out to me, which he obviously was, I mean, hello, then I would have to know the right thing to respond with. I didn't feel ready before, so I excused myself. Was that, like, so incredibly rude and insensitive of me? Will he even tell me now? *Of course he will, Babe, just make him feel fierce, remind him who he is!* Oh my God, I was losing it. Why? I couldn't tell you. It wasn't like *I* was coming out. But I legit needed this to be perfect for him. Clearly it was a HUGE deal for him to get the words out. He was so shockingly cool and comfortable with himself otherwise, but hadn't been able to share this part of himself with anyone UNTIL NOW WTFFFFFFFFFFFFFFF SO MUCH PRESSURE ON ME. Okay. No. Relax.

I quietly sang a few lines of Lady Gaga's "Til It Happens to You," which is about rape, I think, but it worked. I boosted myself up. I was going to be there for him in any way he needed me. I just had to be myself so that he could too.

"Knoxie," I said, sitting back down next to him, "it's really unlike you to hide something from me. Or to hide something from the world, for that matter. It's not on brand for you. I'm just saying. As your manager/mentor, you know?"

"I've just never told anyone this thing I've been thinking about."

"What's the thing?"

"I like someone."

"Fabulous."

"I mean, like, *like* someone."

"Fabulous."

"And it's another boy."

"Fabulous."

Knox looked at me as if it was my turn again to say something, like he was preparing to be scolded or told he was wrong. I wasn't about to do anything of the sort, obvs. We were basically having a staring contest. He finally looked away, and we sat in silence for a few minutes.

"You wanna talk about it?" I asked.

"Not really. I just needed to say that. Don't tell my mom and Cara. I'll do it later."

"Whatever you want, babes."

"Thanks."

I took a sip of my wine, grabbed my magazine, and found the page I'd left off on.

"It's nice you won't have to date girls, actually," I told him. "We can be a shit-show. Especially when we're teenagers."

"Oh . . . okay. Yeah, I guess that's good." Knox agreed, uncomfortably. I think he was in shock. We didn't talk about it any more. He just flipped on a movie and that was that. We just enjoyed our flight as much as we possibly could, knowing that as soon as we landed we were going to face the wrath of a mother scorned. Honestly, I didn't care. I knew I'd done something good for him.

SEVENTEEN
Guess Who Fucked Scott?

"I'm just praying that my mom is so happy for me that she forgets how mad she is."

"Don't you worry about a thing. You are gonna be fine. I kidnapped you. You had literally no choice. I will deal with Veronica."

As the escalator headed down into the depths of the baggage claim area of BWI Airport, I could just make out the figures of Veronica and Cara in the distance. Shockingly, they looked incredibly happy to see us. Thank God Vee was not freaking out. I was completely ready to make my case and explain exactly why I took Knox, but I was thrilled that it seemed like I wouldn't have to.

Veronica and Cara started running toward us, and Knox was equally as excited to see them. They ran at each other and ended up in a group hug. The whole thing made me think of the opening sequence of *Love Actually*. I couldn't tell if it made me hate them all for that moment or if it made me hate myself for being affected by it.

"Mom! I made it. I was picked! They're going to put me on the show! I did the mushrooms that you love and Gordon smiled at me like, a bunch of times and everyone was so nice and LA is weird but so cool!"

"I'm just so relieved that you're back in my arms, safe and sound. We can talk about that later, Knox."

"So pissed you got to go to LA without me," Cara chimed in. She was wearing a jean skirt. No.

"You would have loved it, Cara. I saw famous people. I met Chef Ramsay."

"Hate you."

No one had really looked at me during this whole love-fest so I thought I'd make my presence known.

"He did great," I said. "They really loved him for the show. Totally on brand for them. I think Knox has a real chance of winning it all this season. Based on what his competition looked like. Most of the other little people were in Gap Kids."

It was weird. Veronica was definitely looking at me, but it was more like she looked through me.

"Babe. Don't you dare."

Oh, okay. She was fucking livid. Boy, did I misread this situation.

"Veronica. I'm sorry I took him. I should have talked to you first."

"*You should have talked to me first?* That's what you think would have made this whole thing okay? Babe, you need to come back to reality. You stole my child from my house and took him three thousand miles away without a single word."

So much for not having to explain myself.

"But he needed to be at this audition, Vee. He made the show. I stand by my decision to take him because it obvi paid off in the end. I get that you are upset or whatever that we just snuck away, but you were not even entertaining the idea of letting him go. He is super talented and he deserves a chance to make something of himself. Honestly, it's a miracle that I came into his life when I did and provided him the opportunity."

I knew as soon as the words left my mouth that I'd fucked up. I was tired. It was a fucking red-eye to BWI, give me a break.

"I'm sorry? Are you now insulting the life I can provide for MY son?"

"No. I'm sorry. That's not at all what I meant."

"We're going home. Thank you for not killing my son."

Then Veronica just grabbed Knox, who looked stunned, and they all headed toward the doors.

"Don't you want your luggage?" I yelled. But they didn't turn around. They all kept walking out of the airport, leaving me alone.

"I'm really SORRY!" I yelled in a last-ditch effort to make things right. But they didn't look back. I could see that Knox was trying to stop and turn to say something but they were not letting him. I would've run to him but I don't really run, ever.

I mean . . . I actually kind of get it. Like, I almost see where Veronica is coming from in this situation. Even if she didn't technically give birth to Knox, she still raised him and changed his diapers and all that other terrible stuff that you have to do when you have a baby in your house and there's no Mabinty. I'm sure Mabinty would've cut a bitch for stealing me when I was ten years old. If I was Knox's mom, I would have been totally fucking freaked out if someone took him on a plane trip without asking me first.

Yeah, so actually I completely understand why Veronica just walked out of the airport. She was 1 million percent justified in doing so. I think she will realize, in time, that it was better for Knox that I did take him to the audition. But

I'm gonna let her have her moment. I wonder if she thinks about how she is actually Knox's aunt in these situations. Is it constantly on her mind or has she made peace with it? Donna really just creates havoc wherever she goes. What a slut.

So . . . I was at Baltimore/Washington International Thurgood Marshall Airport at 6:15 a.m., alone. I had a few options: fly back to LA and leave this mess behind me like Donna would do, stay at a hotel in Baltimore (LOL!), or Scott?

Babe Hi!!

Scott Why are you awake?

Babe Why are you awake?

Scott Just heading home from the pool. Where are you?

Babe Scott!!!! DON'T text and drive. You've already died once this week.

Scott That's true. Are you here?

Babe STOP TEXTING.

My phone rang.

"Hi."

"Are you back in Maryland?"

"Yup."

"Was Veronica still upset?"

"Oh, yeah. Piiiiiissed. Can you pick me up?"

"Um . . . where are you?"

"At the airport. I'll drop a pin. United Airlines."

"Where do you need me to take you?"

"I'm not sure. I'm kind of feeling sad. Can you come get me and take me back to your place?"

"Sure. I'll be there in twenty minutes. Try not to make any racist comments to anyone before I get there. K?"

"You know what, never mind. I'll take an Uber to a hotel or just book a flight back to LA."

"Stop. I'm kidding. I was joking at lunch, too, by the way. I don't think you're racist. Which I would have explained if you hadn't freaked out and bolted."

"You're fucking weird, dude."

"So are you, Babe. See you in a few?"

"Yeah."

Scott drove an old Land Rover Defender. Google it. It's one of the only cars on the planet Earth that can actually make a guy hotter. It's like the kind of vehicle you would get if you were going on a safari in Tanzania. It's rugged, not at all flashy, and death is guaranteed if you were ever to get in a wreck in one. I was instantly ten times more attracted to him when he pulled up than I had been when I met him for lunch. Scott gave me a hug when I got in the car. He had Led Zeppelin playing on the car stereo. It was all working for him. Wet hair from the pool. Clean shaven, soapy-smelling, heaven. I really must have wanted to fuck him because I never say or think of the word "heaven," on account of it being sick.

"Was Knox upset that he wasn't able to audition?"

"Oh, he did get to audition. He snuck out of my house in LA yesterday and convinced Mabinty to drive him."

"Wow! Oh my God, that kid. That's pretty crazy. How'd he do?"

"He made it. He's gonna be on the show."

"If Veronica lets him."

"What do you mean?"

"I mean, when she called me freaking out when you first took Knox to LA, she was going on about how she felt like Knox wasn't ready for anything like this."

"That's fucking stupid. He is sooooooooooooooooooo talented. You should've seen how well he was doing at the audition."

"That may be," Scott said. "But I don't think she approves of the whole concept of him being on television. She said that the limelight had already wreaked enough havoc on her family, and that she wasn't about to subject Knox to that whole world."

"I mean . . . I guess? I think that's pretty small-minded. But whatever."

"He's her kid, Babe."

I didn't feel like getting into the whole thing with Scott. Especially not before confronting Veronica about the fact that I had confirmed she wasn't Knox's mom. I felt more torn than ever about whether or not Knox should know the truth. But I at least knew I needed to have a face-to-face with Veronica, without anyone else around. I knew that she would understand where I was coming from about the whole kidnapping if she took a second to listen to me.

It was still only 8 a.m. when we got to Scott's cute little townhouse. It was in Annapolis, which basically looked like a town from the eighteenth century. Colonial or whatever. Quaint, quiet, boring. His house, however, was really nice. Like, super minimal, clean furnishings. Tons of light. Not at all what I pictured. He had some incredible photographs on the walls that he said his sister took. Unclear on that. Scott seemed like he had it all together. I wasn't used to being around a guy who had no "agenda." Scott "was" who he "was" and he wasn't changing that because he was around me. Like the version of yourself that you normally present to someone when you are interested in them is "manufactured" to be more appealing. But this guy didn't know the first thing about that. I liked it.

"You tired?" Scott asked.

"Kind of."

"You can nap in my bed. Door at the top of the stairs."

His house was exceptionally clean, considering he had no idea that I would be with him when he returned to it.

"That's really sweet of you."

"It's fine. Sheets are clean. Fresh towels in the bathroom if you want to wash up."

But I wanted to sleep with him. I really, really wanted to fuck Scott. He'd just rescued me from the airport, and his place wasn't dirty? That equals let's fuck now.

I then had a moment of incredible insecurity.

Scott was not the type of guy that I normally fucked. Most importantly, he didn't care about anything that the guys I normally sleep with care about. He didn't care what kind of car I drove, what clothes I was wearing. He probably wouldn't have noticed that I was a couple of days overdue for a wax. It just made me feel uneasy. Like we were speaking two different languages. But the things that freaked me out about him were the things that made me want him. I just had to own my differences and put myself in the power position. I went from feeling insecure to feeling pretty liberated, actually. Knowing that he didn't really care made me feel completely free.

"I'd like you to come join me for a nap."

"Sure," Scott said, in a completely matter-of-fact way.

"I want to fuck."

"Babe. I can tell when a girl wants to fuck me."

"And?"

"You're hilarious. Yeah. I want to fuck you too."

Then Scott just walked over to me, kissed my neck, and lifted me right off of my feet. I was straddling him and kissing him back. He literally ran up his stairs, threw me on his bed, and ripped his shirt off. He was really in great shape. Swimmer body can sometimes look gross, but not in this case.

When I say that Scott was aggressive, I'm playing it down. He completely dominated me in the bed. Like, out of nowhere. The following words were going through my head on repeat the whole time he was fucking me: *Oh Shit, Oh Shit, Oh Fuck, Oh SHIT*! It was on a loop in my brain. I was being controlled by him. Scott was doing all of the work. I honestly don't even know how big his dick was because we were staring into each other's eyes for almost every second we were in that bedroom. I wouldn't have dared take my eyes off his for one second to catch a glimpse of his peen. It felt biggish inside me, but, like, size actually didn't matter. Whatever size it was was making perfect sense to my vagina. And maybe this is impossible, but I could tell just by the way it felt that it was the perfect shade of pink.

He gave me three ridiculous rocket orgasms. It just never happens, or rarely. We all know how insane that is. So all the claps go to Scott. This was an absolute first for me. Scott gave me the first two without really breaking a sweat—they were gifts. Then on the last one we climaxed together.

"That was really nice, Babe. I like you."

That's what he said to me, with a huge grin on his face, after we finished.

"That was better than nice. That was fucking phenomenal."

"That makes me feel good to hear. I'm starving."

"Me too."

WHO AM I RIGHT NOW?

EIGHTEEN

Babe of Pigs.

"Hi. I'm Babe Walker. I'm here to see Veronica."

"I'm sorry?" said the receptionist at the front desk.

"Babe Walker. Author, friend, philanthropist. I know it's weird that I'm here, but it would take too long for me to explain why so I'm gonna skip that part and just let you deal with the reality of my presence."

She had her hair in the style of a mullet. She didn't look happy.

"Who did you say you were here to see?"

"Veronica. She's a nurse here, right?"

"Are you here to see a patient?"

"No. I'm here to see Veronica. Is there more than one nurse named Veronica that works here?"

"One second, please," she said, picking up an old beige phone and pressing a few buttons on the number pad. "Miss, you can sit down over there. Vee will come get you when she's able to."

"Oh, it's okay, I'll just wait here. I prefer to stand."

"Suit yourself."

I offered her a smile, leaned against the counter, and examined my nails. My navy-blue manicure was chipping, but I was kind of dying for it. The perfect hint of grunge to complement my otherwise neopreppy look: a ribbed Proenza sweater in chartreuse, an asymmetric Maison Rabih Kayrouz miniskirt, and metallic Robert Clergerie espadrille chukka boots. I was giving you mature youth and wise vulnerability.

"This place is wayyyy less disgusting than I thought it would be. No offense at all. I just always imagined assisted-living homes to be more like hospitals. This is, like—"

"Miss?" scowled our Royal Mulletessa de la Front Desk.

"Yes, Queen?" I shot back.

"I have work to do, so you talkin' me up like we're in line at Starbucks waitin' to order our Pumpkin Spice Lattes ain't gonna work, hon."

"I totally understand, and you *are* being heard. But before I walk away and sit over there to wait for my aunt Veronica, I'm going to need confirmation that you understand one thing about me."

"What's that?"

"I have never and will never order a Pumpkin Spice Latte from Starbucks."

She looked at me for a long, awkward amount of time. I felt imprisoned by her blank stare. It was odd. Then she simply pointed to an empty row of chairs against the far wall. I put my bag over my arm and walked over. I called her a whore in my mind.

As I sat down it occurred to me that at one point in my life, not too long prior, I would've just called her a whore out loud, caused a scene, slapped someone, and I probably would've just left without talking to Vee. I wasn't sure if containing my emotions and exhibiting some restraint for the sake of the greater good made me a better person or a more boring person. On one hand—

"Babe?" I heard Vee's voice say.

"Heyyyyyy . . ." I said, my voice trailing off slowly into a low "ehhhhyyyy." Not cute.

"What are you doing here?"

"I wanted to talk to you."

"What do we have to talk about?"

"A lot," I said, standing my ground. I wasn't going any-where. Knox needed us to have this conversation, so have this conversation we would.

"Okay. Give me, like, fifteen, and we can talk outside. I've gotta wrap something up."

"Love it. Go save some people. You're an inspiration," I offered, trying to be nice.

She rolled her eyes and walked away. Without turning back to face me she just said, "Outside by the garden in fif-teen," and the saloon doors flapped closed behind her.

I wasn't going to wait outside and be sweaty for our meeting so I decided just to wait here and meditate a little bit. I shut my eyes and positioned my hands in an open lotus mudra (that's Sanskrit for "hand pose") and just let my mind run wild. I found myself atop a Himalayan moun-tain peak, standing stark naked at the edge of a sheer cliff, weathering the blustering winds with grace and fortitude. Floating past me, or swimming, rather, were extremely small pigs. And when I say small I mean they were like fit-in-the-palm-of-your-hand small. Thousands of them swimming through the air. Some pink, some black, some a marbly mix of pig skin tones, all kicking their little feet through the icy textures of the storm. It was a wonder to see, really. The color story was gorgeous. It was reminiscent of Chanel's aviation/airport-themed Spring/Summer 2016 show. (Not

clear on that show or that collection, BTW.) I felt so connected to the airborne swine that I had the urge to step off
the cliff and join their migration. As I shifted my weight to
step off, I felt a tap on my knee.

The tap wasn't in my meditation.

I opened my eyes and saw an old woman was sitting
next to me. She was tapping my knee. We were now looking
right at each other. I was clearly responding to her, yet she
was still tap-tap-tapping on my li'l knee.

"Can I help you?" I asked, glancing at the clock on the
wall across from us in hopes that I'd been meditating for
almost fifteen minutes, meaning I could excuse myself for
my meeting with Veronica. It had been one minute.

"You know," she said in old-lady voice that might've
been slightly southern, "I don't want to bother you."

"You're not," I lied.

"But I was on my way outside to have a check on my
lilies and I couldn't help but see you settin' here all alone
lookin' so damn pretty with your little eyes closed and all
this gorgeous hair."

I decided I liked her.

"And I know he doesn't like me doing this," she continued, "but my grandson . . . Here, let me show you a picture."

She pulled an iPhone 6 Plus out from a pocket in her polar
fleece jacket and before I even go on I want to acknowledge

two insane things: 1) This lovely old bitty was wearing a fleece jacket to walk outside into an unusually humid May day, and 2) She was at least 112 years old and had the same phone as me.

As if she wasn't senile, she slid her phone unlocked and searched through her photos, by date and location, mind you, to find a photo of her grandson. Maybe she wasn't senile? But she looked so old. And she said "settin'" instead of "sitting." But it was possible that she was totally with it like my Tai Tai had been, may she rest in peace. Loved that for her.

"Here he is. Jimmy," she said, presenting her phone to me. On the screen was a photo of an average white male between the ages of twenty-five and thirty-five. He did have gorgeous eyes. They were eyes with a secret—I could tell he was a freak. He was sweating and wearing a running outfit with some sort of piece of paper clipped to his chest. It looked like he'd just finished running a marathon. I wondered if his nipples bled during the run; I've heard that can happen.

"Oh, wow," I said, feigning excitement. "That's great that he's, like, in shape and stuff."

"Quite handsome, isn't he? He's the sweetest boy in the world, I'm tellin' ya."

"And what? He's single?"

"He is single! Can you even believe it?"

"No. I'm shocked."

"We're all shocked. And Jesus, is he a catch! He's an accountant and he's very, very good with money. You live around here?" she asked.

"No. I'm not from here. I honestly don't even know where I am right now."

She just smiled and nodded, confused.

"And besides, I just kinda started seeing someone. I'm not in the best place to be sleeping with new people right now, to be completely fucking honest. And you're sweet for asking, really. But—"

I stopped talking. It occurred to me what I'd just said to her. The fuck? Did I just refer to Scott as someone I'd kinda started seeing? Where did that come from? I guess I liked him. But, like . . . what? No.

"I'm sorry," I said, getting up from my seat. "You're an angel and I love that you want me to marry into your wonderfully normal family, but I need to go."

"Oh. Oh, yeah, sure. I'm sorry if I bothered you."

"You didn't. I'm just a bitch and when I get uncomfortable I stand up and leave."

Smiles, nods, confusion. I smiled back and went to wait for Vee on the bench outside. One Marlboro Light later, Vee was sitting with me. I hadn't noticed before, but she was wearing scrubs with little animals printed all over. I refrained from telling her how I felt about this entire concept. I had the foresight to know that that wasn't the best way to start this particular convo.

"I've only got about ten minutes. We had two major tumbles today so a couple of very fragile ladies are in need of extra care and we're understaffed, as per usual."

"I'll be quick."

"Okay. What's up?"

"I guess if you don't have much time then I should just get right to it."

"That sounds like a good plan," Vee said, not really putting up with one minute of my shit.

"Okay, I know you're upset with me for taking Knox to LA, but I need you to know that I fucking love that kid, Vee. I only want what's best for him. I've never cared about anyone like this, I swear. So I'm figuring out how to be a good role model and it's weird and I get carried away and get drunk and fly to LA sometimes, but I'm learning, I swear."

"You know what, Babe? I get it. You think you can come in and be a hero for Knox or whatever, but he is a kid. He's a ten-year-old boy with a perfectly happy and safe life here. Do you not understand that? And he's been acting differently since you got here."

"Yeah, he's been happy. He's been so extremely happy and driven that he took it upon himself to make it to that audition and follow his dream of being a MasterChef! That's a big deal, Veronica."

She shook her head like I was only pissing her off the more I said.

"I won't sit here and have you talk about my son like you're his mother."

"I know I'm not his mother, you psycho! But I'm his sister, and that's worth something."

"What did you say?"

"Oh, please, I've known since the birthday party. Your dad told me, and I confirmed it from another extremely reliable source in California."

"Did you tell him?" she asked, terrified.

"I would never. But keeping this pot of boiling-hot truth-tea from him has literally been making me sick. I can't do it. I can't."

"You think it's been hard for you? I've lived with this for ten years."

"And honestly, Vee, I think you are probably the world's most amaze mom for how you've raised him. I don't wanna fuck that up. I just want him to know the truth and honestly I think he can handle it. He's literally a grown woman in his head. He's not really a ten-year-old boy, you get that, right? He's Padma Lakshmi. He's Grace Coddington. He can handle the truth!"

"Who are they?"

"The point is I think we need to tell him."

Vee put her head in her hands and smoothed her hair back.

"You want to know why I've never told him? Why I've kept the truth about his birth mother from him for so long?" she asked, but I didn't get the sense she wanted me to answer. "Because I wanted to protect him from Donna. I saw what she did with you and I know you ended up doing okay for yourself and your dad has you all set up out there in California, but it got to a point where he was too sweet and too smart and too special for me to then tell him that this horrible, selfish woman was the person who brought him into this world and not me. I know if I open up that door then she'll find ways to hurt him. She'll either deny all of it and run away again or pretend like she's gonna be a part of his life and just end up disappointing him. I won't let her hurt him. I won't do it."

I didn't realize right away, but by the time Veronica stopped talking, I was crying. She pulled a pack of tissues out of her scrubs and gave me one.

"Thanks," I said, barely getting it out. "Fuck me. This is intense. You're right. I hadn't even thought about the Donna of it all."

"I know you hadn't. Donna is a deeply unhappy person. Like, she is fucked up and she leaves a path of destruction everywhere she goes. I've known her longer than you. I know who she really is, not the person she takes photos as. I've always told my dad that."

"What?"

"That she wouldn't be a good model if she knew how to be a decent, loving, or even kind person. She wouldn't be so cutthroat. She'd make time for people. She'd care about others and their time. It took a lot of fucking people over and being a shark to get where she did. She wasn't plucked off a horse as a ten-year-old like Christy Turlington. Donna made her*self*."

"First of all, obsessed that you know how Christy Turlington's career started, and also, I know what you're saying. Like, I hate it and it's weird and a little sad for me because she is my mom at the end of the day, but I get it. I totally get it."

"Good."

"And I wouldn't want Knox to have to have some of the thoughts I've had about her. I mean, I normally don't give a fuck about what she's doing/saying/snorting, but the dark truth is, I'd be better off if I grew up with a real mom. I know that."

"And when you took Knox from me—"

"I didn't take him from you."

"Babe, you literally kidnapped him. But you know what I mean. It scared the living shit out of me. I don't know you, Babe. I don't know what you're actually like, what you stand for, what matters to you, if you know how to handle kids. All I really know about you are the things I've heard on the news and that you're Donna's kid. And if you're anything like my sister, if you see the world like she does . . ."

Vee started to cry too. Now it was fucking ridiculous. Such a CW show.

"I get it," I said and I took her hand and just held it for a few seconds. I have NEVER in my life. I don't console, I just don't, but I wasn't me. "I'm not my mom. Well, really Mabinty Jones is my mom, and I kind of am hers, but that's beside the point. I won't abandon Knox like she did. I swear on Isabella Blow's grave."

"Who?" Vee said between sniffles.

"Forget it."

She laughed. I lit a cigarette. She asked for a drag, and I gladly gave her one.

"I don't smoke," she said after a long, professional pull and exhale.

"Of course you don't. Then you'll probably want to finish that one."

"Thanks," she said. I gave it a few minutes and let her

enjoy her cigarette, which she smoked like it was her last day on earth.

"Veronica?"

"What? I should go back inside. I gotta get back."

"We're gonna talk to him before I leave. Like, it has to happen."

"I know."

"I'll come over tonight when your shift is over. Will Knox be home or does he have a lesson or something annoying?"

"Sure. Come by at six. I'll make some food for us, and we can talk to him."

"Okay, chic. I'm not gonna eat, but great, sounds perf."

"Is this really the best thing for him?" she asked me with real despair in her voice.

"One trillion percent," I confirmed.

"Can you believe I'm asking you for advice?"

"Yes."

"Right. Of course you can."

"And while we're on the subject of me knowing what to do: you gotta let him do the show. He's a fucking star. You didn't need to be there at that audition to know how ecstatic he was. I know you know how much he wanted that."

"Of course I know."

"So let him live. It doesn't have to be scary; it *can* be a good thing, I promise. We'll be by his side keeping him in check."

"No, I'll be keeping him in check, and you'll be buying him designer clothes and taking him to hotel parties."

"Never again! I learned my lesson. But, like, to be totally honest, if we use Drew as an example, she was blowing rails of coke and, like, fucking E.T. when she was nine or whatever and look at her now: wholesome mom vibes as fuck."

"Drew Barrymore?"

"No, Drew Carey. Yes, Drew Barrymore, hello?"

"Not funny, Babe."

"I wasn't trying to be funny. So . . . thanks?"

She shook her head, chucked the cigarette butt to the side, smoothed the top of her horrible pants down with her hands, and stood up.

"I'll think about the show," she said with a tiny smirk.

That was all I needed.

As Vee walked away, I caught another glimpse of the print on her scrubs. I hadn't noticed before but the tiny animal cartoons were all of pigs and they were drawn as if they were barreling through space. Pigs of all different colors. Just like my vision. I bit my lip and pondered the great connectivity of our majestic and spiritually aligned planet. And then I said, "LOL," out loud.

NINETEEN

Can We Finish Our Salads Now?

As I'd expected, Veronica didn't cook shit for dinner, Knox did. And it looked gorgeous but being around him for the past week and a half was like living inside a chic Food Network show, and I'd been eating in a manner that was entirely excessive and out of character. So, much to Knox's dismay, she was gonna need to juice for a while. She being me.

When I got to the house, Knox was obviously thrilled to see me. When he went into the kitchen to finish dinner, Vee pulled me aside and let me know that Cara was going to a friend's house for dinner, which was her preference anyway because she planned on telling Cara about Donnagate separately. I told her that was wise because Cara's a fucking bitch and she'd definitely say something rude to spoil the sensitive moment. Vee didn't disagree, but she was mad that I called Cara a bitch, and I told her she was just mad because it's true.

I did get to say hi to the angsty princess before she left. She came down from her room in an outfit that can only be described as "how?" but I did my best to hide my shock. Can someone please explain to me why kidnapping Knox was such a big deal to Vee, but she has no qualms letting her only daughter leave the house in pleather H&M boy shorts, an oversized hoodie with the words "Text Me Never" emblazoned across the chest as if they were spray-painted there, and a pair of extremely dirty brown Ugg boots?

Cara stood at the bottom of the stairs holding her phone, hair up in a side-pony.

"You're still here?" she said.

"Actually, no. This is just a hologram of Babe Walker that your mom had installed in the house so I could be with you guys forever and always," I served back.

"I know that's not true because we can't afford a holographic projector. I asked my mom for one last Christmas."

"What? Really? Why?"

"I wanted a hologram of Justin in my room so I could learn the choreography to his videos."

"Bieber?"

"No Timberlake . . . Yes, Bieber, hello?"

"Ew. I mean, they make a Justin Bieber hologram machine?"

"No. But I still asked for it."

"Oh, in that case I respect your creativity in gift requests. Not everyone has that."

"I don't even know what that means, but okay," Cara said, flipping her ponytail around to the other shoulder and walking toward her mom's room. "Mommmmmmmmmmmm! I'm gonna wait outside for Lizzie and her mom."

"Okay!" Vee shouted from her room. "Text me when you get there, K?"

"I always do!"

And Cara was out the door. The screaming back and forth was a lot for me, so much that I didn't even think to say good-bye to Cara. I didn't know if I'd ever see Cara again. I mean, I knew I probably would, but I didn't necessarily *need* to, so I knew I wouldn't for a long time. I should've at least said bye.

I walked into the kitchen where Knox was making salad dressing, or that's what it looked like.

"Hey," he said when he saw me, "can you just mix this around till you think it's good?"

"Sure," I said, taking the little metal bowl and spoon from him. I'd never done this job before so it was a fun new experience for me.

"I think you're gonna want to eat what I made."

"I think I'm not."

"Rude!"

"You'll get over it. What *are* you making?" I asked, knowing full well I was having my juice for dinner.

"Here," he said, walking over to a big wooden bowl at the corner of the counter, "I'll show you and you tell me if you think it looks right."

"If it looks right?"

He carried the bowl over and put it in front of me. Inside the bowl was an exact replica of my favorite salad in the entire universe: the La Scala Chopped Salad. It was uncanny. Every ingredient was chopped within the right dimensions, and the proportions were spot on. I almost screamed but stopped myself because I don't scream about food. But I wanted to.

"What!? How?!"

"I've been wanting to try this salad since reading about it in your book and since we never got the chance to go to the, like, real La Scala when we were in LA, I figured I would just make it for you here. And also this way I can try it."

"Knox. It's breathtaking."

"So you'll eat it with us?"

I paused. Contemplated. Looked down at Knox, who

was now making the most adorbs exaggerated frowny bitch-boy face at me.

"I'm gonna have some, yes. It would be my honor," I said.

"Wooo!"

"What are you wooooing about?" Vee said, walking into the kitchen. She'd put on a bit of tinted moisturizer or foundation because she looked fresh.

"Babe's eating the salad," Knox announced.

"Honey, you know we shouldn't celebrate the fact that Babe has extreme food issues, right?"

"Mom, I'm celebrating the fact that she's eating."

"All right," she said, rolling her eyes in the same way she always did: naturally and without care for my feelings.

"He made me my favorite salad. I'm pausing my cleanse for the next hour."

"Then I guess we should sit down," Vee said. She seemed genuinely happy and not nearly as nervous as I was about the conversation we were about to have.

"You guys sit," said Knox, frantically. "I'm gonna go put on a different shirt. Babe, can you take the salad out?"

He ran upstairs. Vee and I sat across from each other, leaving the space between us at the head of the table for Knox.

"Why aren't you nervous?" I whispered.

"I'm fucking terrified, are you kidding??" she hissed back.

"You're hiding it really well."

"Yeah, well, I'm good at hiding things."

I liked that she said that. It calmed me down for some reason. I told myself that it was going to be fine. Knox would be okay. I'd spent the last few days arguing how strong he was, but in this moment I wasn't able to convince even myself. But Veronica and I were in this together, which was weird. We were like Knoxie's lesbian moms. She was Annette Bening, and I was totally Julianne Moore. But, like, she's my aunt, which makes this fantasy interesting.

Anyway.

Knox entered proudly in one of the polos I bought him.

"Yas, queen!" I squealed upon his return.

The smile Veronica shot me let me know that he'd come out to her, too. She knew, she supported, she loved. I almost started crying again. I was getting sick of this emotionally raw thing. Like, enough.

I raised the glass of rosé that Vee had brought to the table for me.

"Can I just say, you both look super cute tonight."

"Thanks, Babe!" Knox said.

"Veronica," I continued, "you're wearing makeup and it's major."

"I figured why not."

"Let me serve you guys," I said, standing up and grabbing the two wooden serving spoons. I proceeded to load all of our plates with pure salad heaven. Serving people: another entirely new activity for me.

We all got into our salads pretty hard as soon as I sat back down. It was so good to be sort of back at La Scala—I missed my safe space.

"When are you gonna decide about the show, Mom? I know you're gonna say no. But I've prepared a formal statement that I'd love the opportunity to present to you so that I can hopefully sway your decision," Knox said to Vee before taking a huge bite of salad.

"We will talk about that. But I wanted to talk to you about something else first, okay?"

"Yeah, sure, what? But can it be a short conversation, because I think the show is probably more important."

"Okay, now hear me out," Vee said, gathering herself. "I know the last week or so has been pretty crazy around here and a lot has happened. I was obviously pretty upset about some things that happened with Babe and your trip to LA, but she came by the center today and we talked through all of that. She's not necessarily the helpless mess that I'd pinned her as."

"I'm sitting literally right here."

"I don't really care," Vee said, turning to me. "That's what I thought. I had every reason to."

"Wrong. But fair," I conceded. "Go on."

"And we talked about something that's come up for her since she came here. And before I really get into this, honey I want you to know a few things. Okay?"

"Sure," Knox said, plainly.

"Knoxie," she said, welling up, "if someone were to ask what mattered most to me in this world, I would tell them my son, Knox."

"I know, Mom. I love you too. Why are you sad?"

"I'm not sad. I'm not sad at all. I'm so insanely proud of the person you are. You're not like anyone else on this planet, I'm sure of it. You may only have ten years under your belt, but I know your spirit is much, much older than that. I've encouraged you to be who you are, I always have, but you have yourself to thank for who that kid is. You're really brave, Knoxie. And you know how I have bad days sometimes, and it's hard for me to get up and get to work or make dinner or whatever it is that day?"

"Yeah, Mom, I know."

"Well, you're the reason I'm able to do it. You're not going to believe me, and God I wish I said this to you more often, but you remind me that it's all going to be okay. So with that in mind . . ."

Veronica took a deep breath and a shaky-handed sip of her wine.

". . . I need to tell you something about our family. But I need you to know that everything *really* will be okay and nothing, absolutely nothing, is going to change."

"Jesus shit, can you just get to it already?" I blurted.

They both looked at me. Knox laughed uncomfortably, Vee rolled her eyes.

"Knox," she said, "when you were born—"

"Oh, this?" he said.

Vee shot me a look of worry, then back to Knox.

"I don't think you know what I'm—"

"Donna's my mom. I know. Two years ago at one of Cara's spelling bees, I overheard Grandpa Joe say something about Donna being a repeat offender or something and that one day I'd find out, so I figured it out on my own."

I was speechless. Veronica looked dead.

"So yeah. I didn't know what 'repeat offender' meant. I Googled it and was still pretty confused but didn't ask any questions because it didn't seem to be important. It wasn't something we'd ever talked about in our house or anything. But then I read your book, Babe. Yeah, that's what happened. And it made sense to me then."

"Oh my God, Knox baby," Vee said to him, taking his little hand across the table.

"I'm fine. I mean, you're my mom, not Donna. Donna's crazy."

"Oh my GOD! You knew?" I wailed and a wall of ugly tears came rushing out of me. "This shit is too much, I'm sorry. Knox, I love you so much."

"I guess I didn't, like, actually *know* until right now, but I was pretty sure."

"I can't believe this," Vee said, shaking her head incessantly. I couldn't tell if she was mad or relieved. I was just trying to keep it together and failing.

"Also, Mom, I sent a strand of Cara's hair and a strand of my hair to this website that does DNA testing and found out that she wasn't my biological sister or whatever, which didn't really surprise me."

We all burst into laughter—that type of uproar that can only come from a group of nervous psychos who need DESPERATELY to laugh.

"Babe, I wanted it to be true. I knew it would be. But ever since I met you and you were so nice to me and you liked me and the way I dressed and how I talked . . . I don't know, I thought if I brought it up, it might freak you out and you might not want to hang out with me and help me with my cooking and everything."

I wiped my eyes and blew my nose into my paper towel napkin. A third thing I'd never done before.

"You can't freak me out. We're family, Knoxie. The only thing that would freak me out would be if you stopped being a freak."

"Hey, I'm not a freak!" he said, pointing at me and smiling. "You're a freak! You got plastic surgery on your vagina!"

"KNOX!!!" shouted Veronica, her face turning red.

"Sorry, Mom."

"It's true," I told her. "I got a labiaplasty for my graduation from high school. And I'm extremely proud of it."

"Jesus Christ."

"It's a beautiful vagina now. I used to have major issues with it but now—"

"Okay, okay!" Vee said, silencing me. "We obviously have a lot to talk about, but maybe tonight's already been emotional enough . . . But are you okay, Knoxie? You know that you're *my* son, you're *my* baby. You know that, right? You always will be."

"Oh my God, Mom. Really?? Yes, I get it!"

It was truly shocking how much Knox was me.

"Okay," Vee said, throwing her hands up, as shocked as I was by his composure through all of this but accepting it as best she could.

"Can we finish our salads now?" Knox asked after about a minute of heavy sighs and under-her-breath "oh my Gods" from Veronica.

"Yeah, let's do that," she agreed.

I lifted my glass to make another toast.

"So here's to us being so fucking cute and chic and open with each other."

We cheers'd.

"And also, she brought us all together, but it needs to be said: fuck Donna."

"Fuck Donna!" the three of us said in unison. It felt amazing. It felt amazing and weird.

TWENTY

Bye.

FROM: Babe Walker (Babe@BabeWalker.com)
TO: Donna Valeo (d.valeo7979@gmail.com)
SUBJECT: HEYYYYYYYY!

Donna—

It's been a few months since we last saw each other in Maryland. I trust that you've been up to your usual antics and that all is well with you and Gina. You looked fab in MD, and it genuinely gives me hope about the aging process. I waited until I'd had time to process all the changes in my life before I wrote you this note. But I've been thinking about writing it every day for the past four months. So get your oolong tea and your pack of American Spirits, I have a lot to say.

First and foremost, thanks for inviting me to Joe's birthday thing. It was truly one of the most eye-opening experiences I've ever had. Even more than squirrel diving. I was not expecting much because our relationship is weird, so I figured it would just be a lot of that: weird and awk interactions with people I don't know but should. I think I was hoping to catch up with you a bit and get to know you a little better, but that didn't happen because that's never going to happen. That's okay, though. I did, however, learn a ton about myself on that trip. Most importantly I learned that I'm not an only child. Which until this spring was one of my defining attributes as a human being. But as it turns out, you gave me the best gift of all but somehow managed to forget to tell me. I have a brother! This is MAJOR news. Soooo exciting, right?? Why didn't you tell me? You're so silly, Donna.

Knox is amazing. He blows me away every single day that I'm with him. I gather from Veronica that you haven't checked in on him for a while so let me give you the full update on our little Knoxy pants. I kidnapped him for a couple of days in May so we could fly to LA to audition for a kids' cooking competition reality show. Veronica was super pissed because I didn't get her permission about taking him, but we worked through it and Knox made it onto the show so I think that made it a lot easier to see how important it really was. Knox came back out to LA to do the show right after school ended in June. They flew him out here a little early and he stayed with Dad, Mabinty, and me at the house. It was amazing. They all loved him, my friends all loved him. He really is an amazing kid. He made it to the fourth round of the show before getting kicked off. It was actually a real shame. Some other greasy kid on his team totally overcooked the Pumpkin Ravioli, and Knox got blamed because he was the team leader for the challenge that week.

But it doesn't really matter because he stole the show every time he was on camera. Gordon Ramsay, who dad represents, already told Knox that he could have a job at one of his restaurants as soon as he is old enough. Knox is beyond thrilled, obviously. He idolizes Gordon. Knox was so great about getting kicked off the show. He is so mature. I assume he gets it from his dad? Who is his dad anyway? Genuinely curious about that.

Also, Knox knows the truth. He has for a while. Joe had mentioned something to him, so he was already suspicious, but he got the official proof and kept it to himself. Love him for that. It's pretty remarkable what well-adjusted kids you produce. Especially since you're a ghost in all of their lives. Maybe it's *because* you aren't around that we're doing so well.

Knox just left this morning back to Maryland. I miss him already. But we made a pact to not go more than two months without seeing each other. I'm already planning to take him to NYC for fashion week next month. He loves fashion. Kylie Jenner is one of his style icons, which wouldn't be my pick, but I'm letting him live. Then we will probably do Thanksgiving together. I'm kind of seeing one of the teachers from Cara and Knox's school. His name is Scott. He is hot and he makes going to Maryland cuter for sure. Love Knox, obvi, but I'd definitely be trying to get him out to LA more if it weren't for Scott. Plus, I think it's better for Veronica that I come there more. She is his mom, after all.

For as long as I can remember, I've always felt like I was the kind of person that might never settle down. I always get close, but then something scares me away because on some level I believed that I just wasn't gonna be good in a family situation. Maybe I was making it okay for you to have behaved in the way that you did, by pretending that I was that way, too. Pretending that I couldn't commit to anything or anyone. But I know now that that isn't the case. That's not who I am. I'm not really like you at all. And that's okay. It's okay you weren't there for me and that you weren't there for Knox. We have each other now. And that's just as good for us. I wouldn't trade it for anything.

It turns out that family (as a concept) isn't as fucked up as I thought. In fact, family isn't really that fucked up at all. I guess what I'm saying is that you're a bad mom. You should know that. But that doesn't mean that I'm going to be one. That has been my biggest fear about settling down and starting my own family. But being with Knox these past few months has given me a glimpse into what motherhood is all about. I honestly see how much you have to be there for another human being. Watching Veronica with Knox has been a beautiful lesson in the right way to be someone's mother. Everything she does, she does for those kids. She has no taste whatsoever and her hair is always a fucking mess, but her heart is, like, the biggest heart. She actually reminds me of Meryl

Streep. She is completely focused on her kids' well-being. And somehow . . . that's attractive to me all of a sudden. I guess it's the new me? My dad's new wife is actually proud of me. She says I've transformed over the past few months. I think transformation is bullshit but I'll take it as a compliment.

So I'm down one mom, but up one brother. But I'm happy with what I ended up with.

Good luck with everything. I hope this email didn't upset you too much. That wasn't my intention. But I'm sure you'll get over it if it did. 'Cause you're a cunt.

Sincerely,

B

FROM: Babe Walker (Babe@BabeWalker.com)
TO: Lizbeth (liz@lizbethprod.com)
SUBJECT: Mantra

How is St. Barths? Are you guys ever coming back to LA? You can tell my dad that his new Rolex came. Also tell him that I miss him. You can tell yourself that I miss you too if you want. Which is kind of what I'm writing to you about. I've had some time now to digest this whole situation with my bio mom. And I guess all the bullshit led me to realize what my mantra was, in a way.

You don't have to be someone's mother to be their, like, mother.

It hit me like a ton of bricks, in the middle of a Flywheel class, and then I just sat on the bike for the last half hour of the class staring into space and repeating the mantra over and over. It's actually perfect for me. On two levels. First and foremost, this mantra allows me to own some of the motherly responsibilities I've been taking on with Knox. I'm obvi not his mom, but I also kind of am, you know? And I'm okay with it. Maybe I do want to be a mom after all.

Also . . . it made me reexamine my often tense, normally horrible relationship with you. So I kind of get that you aren't really trying to be my mom, but you also aren't trying not to be my mom. And I appreciate it, Lizbeth. I really do.

XO

B

EPILOGUE

So . . . Even though Knox didn't win the show, the country was basically obsessed with him after he was on. So it was not hard for me to help him get a book deal for a cookbook with his recipes. I've taken the liberty of including some of my faves for you guys to enjoy. (Please note that I've also made some small changes to these recipes to make them more organic, lower-cal, and just healthier all around.)

Bon appétit.

~~POTATO AND~~ ONION FRITTATA

SERVES 6

INGREDIENTS

12 Whole Eggs

~~4 Yukon Gold Potatoes, sliced thin~~ (Um... No potatoes, please)

1 White Onion, sliced thin

¼ Cup Extra Virgin Olive Oil

~~2 T Kosher Salt~~ (Skip the salt unless you want to be puffy AF)

INSTRUCTIONS

Preheat oven to 350 degrees F.

In large bowl, whisk eggs until well combined.

Heat sloped-sided pan to med. high heat, add half the oil, ~~and sauteé potatoes until tender, remove with a slotted spoon and add to egg mixture.~~ Add onions to pan and fry until golden and tender, remove, and transfer to egg mixture. Add remaining oil to pan, and pour in egg mixture. Stir eggs quickly until some curds form. Place in oven, bake 10–20 minutes, remove when eggs have risen and are golden brown. Serve directly from skillet.

BANANA-GRAIN PANCAKE

SERVES 4

DRY INGREDIENTS

½ Cup of Buckwheat Flour

½ Cup of Millet Flour

½ Cup of Quinoa Flour

½ Cup of Tapioca Starch

1 T of Baking Powder

WET INGREDIENTS

1 Over-ripened Banana

¼ Cup Sugar

¼ Cup Greek Yogurt

¼ Cup Water

2 T Coconut Oil

2 Whole Eggs

~~Pinch Salt~~

INSTRUCTIONS

Mix dry ingredients together in a large bowl. In separate bowl combine banana with sugar and salt, mash with fork. Whisk in remaining wet ingredients until smooth and well combined. Combine wet and dry ingredients. Heat skillet to med. heat. Add oil. Ladle in pancake mixture and cook on both sides 2–3 minutes per side until golden brown and slightly risen. Serve with maple syrup and crème fraîche.

SUMMER GAZPACHO

SERVES 6

(LOVE this one. Although I've found it actually makes 24 hearty and filling portions for me.)

INGREDIENTS

2 lbs. Heirloom Tomatoes, diced

1 Green Bell Pepper, diced

1 Cucumber, peeled, seeds removed, diced

1 Garlic Clove

½ Red Onion, diced

½ Loaf Country Bread, crust removed, diced

~~4 T Kosher Salt~~ *(1 Tablespoon is plenty)*

2 T Sherry Vinegar

⅓ Cup Extra Virgin Olive Oil

INSTRUCTIONS

Combine all ingredients, except for sherry vinegar and olive oil, in large bowl, cover, and let sit for a few hours or overnight in the fridge. Blend the mixture in blender until smooth. Add olive oil and sherry vinegar and blend until combined. Serve chilled.

SEARED CHICKEN WITH FENNEL SALAD

SERVES 4

INGREDIENTS

4 Chicken Thighs, bone in, skin on, organic

2 T Canola Oil

~~4 T Kosher Salt~~

1 T Black Pepper, ground

3 Fennel Bulb, core removed, sliced very thin

1 Meyer Lemon, or Regular Lemon

4 T Extra Virgin Olive Oil

1 T Sea Salt

INSTRUCTIONS

Preheat oven to 375 degrees F.

Heat large skillet, cast iron if you have it, to med. high heat. Add canola oil and let it get hot. Season chicken on both sides with ~~kosher salt and~~ black pepper. Add chicken to skillet, skin side down. Bring heat to medium and let the skin sear for 8 minutes until golden brown and crispy. Turn chicken over, and put whole skillet in oven. Bake until done, about 6–10 minutes.

While chicken is in oven, place sliced fennel in large bowl, zest the lemon directly over the fennel. ~~Season with salt and~~ toss with olive oil and juice from the lemon. Serve beside the seared chicken.

ROASTED SCALLOPS WITH PINE NUTS
~~AND BROWN BUTTER~~

SERVES 4

INGREDIENTS

16 U/10 Scallops

4 T Canola Oil

~~4 T Kosher Salt~~

~~1 lb. Butter, unsalted~~ (STOP suggesting butter, Knox)

1 Cup Pine Nuts, toasted

2 T Sherry Vinegar, aged

INSTRUCTIONS

Heat oven to 350 degrees F.

Heat large skillet to med. high heat. Add canola oil and let it get hot. ~~Season the scallops with salt, and~~ sear scallops in the pan on both sides 2–3 minutes per side. Take out of pan and place onto baking sheet. ~~Place the butter in pan and let it melt, swirl the pan occasionally until the butter starts to turn light brown.~~ Add the vinegar ~~and remaining salt~~ and whisk. Place scallops in the oven for 2–3 minutes until warmed through, remove, and place on the plate. Spoon sauce onto plate and sprinkle with pine nuts.

ORANGE BREAD PUDDING

(LOL. I let him keep this in here because he begged me to. Knox says it's his best recipe. I tried it. Just a bite. It was the best thing I've ever tasted so I had to let it slide. Enjoy/Sorry!)

SERVES 6

INGREDIENTS

½ Loaf Pain de Mie, or Brioche, cubed

2 Cups Whole Milk

3 Whole Eggs, beaten

2 Oranges

⅓ Cup Sugar

2 T Butter

1 Pinch Kosher Salt

INSTRUCTIONS

Preheat oven to 350 degrees F.

Zest the two oranges, and reserve the oranges for other use.

Bring milk, butter, sugar, zest, and salt to a simmer in large-capacity pot. Simmer just until sugar dissolves. Whisk in the eggs and pour mixture over bread in large bowl. Let soak for a few hours. Transfer mixture to greased baking dish. Bake in oven for 25–30 minutes. Remove when the mixture has risen and is no longer wobbly. Serve with vanilla ice cream.

ACKNOWLEDGMENTS

I used to hate saying thanks for anything. I thought it made me look needy. But I've learned to own my neediness. It's part of me. It's my thing. I am an extremely needy person and that's just what it is. So, I NEED to thank a few people without whom this book would not have been possible and also my life would fucking suck.

Ninety-nine percent of the people I meet are literal garbage, but there a few that I truly do love, besides myself: Tanner Cohen and David Oliver Cohen, you guys complete me. Like actually, how would I have written this book without you? Thank you, thank you, thank you! Knox, thanks for doing you and inspiring me to do me, and Cara, thanks for letting me burn your Snuggie. I also legit owe so much to Vee for dealing with the shenanigans and accepting that I just might be a better mother figure to Knox than you are—just kidding. I even want to thank Donna, but not for anything she did, more for everything she never did; it shaped me into the eternally blossoming lotus that I am. Thanks, Dad, you are my Queen forever, and Lizbeth, I have to say I've really learned to love your bullshit antics and posi-vibes. It's weird. Thanks to Scott and all the other guys I've fucked lately; it's been a really nice, long stretch of good sex, so thank you, seriously. Thanks to my hot agent, Byrd, for being the first person who believed in me as an author besides my own dad, who doesn't count as a person really, and to my editor, Kate Dresser, you are a true ride-or-die psycho for me and I love you for that. To Jen Bergstrom and Louise Burke and entire team at Gallery, I fuck with you so hard.

Additionally I want to thank Gen Larson, Roman, Mabinty Jones, Cristi Andrews Cohen, Hal Winter, Penelope Ziggy, Jessica Lindsey, Luce Amelia, Marcia and Stewart Cohen, Liz and Frank Newman, Jake Brodsky, Beige, Audrey Adams, Cow, Sam Wilkes, Alex Ferzan, Josh Ostrovsky, Steph Krasnoff, Olivia Wolfe, George Clinton and

P-Funk, the entire cast of Nickelodeon's *Taina*, Tom Cruise, Penelope Cruz, Hazel Judd, Monica Vinny, the Rosé boys, the #1 donkey in the life, Gordon Ramsay, Taylor Bell, Jason Richman, Howie Sanders, Scott Waxman, and Meryl Streep.